Dancing with Shadows and Other Stories

Olabisi Gwamna

Hamilton Books
A member of
The Rowman & Littlefield Publishing Group
Lanham • Boulder • New York • Toronto • Plymouth, UK

Copyright © 2008 by
Hamilton Books
4501 Forbes Boulevard
Suite 200
Lanham, Maryland 20706
Hamilton Books Acquisitions Department (301) 459-3366

Estover Road
Plymouth PL6 7PY
United Kingdom

Library of Congress Control Number: 2007933730
ISBN-13: 978-0-7618-3853-1 (paperback : alk. paper)
ISBN-10: 0-7618-3853-8 (paperback : alk. paper)

Table of Contents

Dancing With Shadows

The people sat in clusters around the large viewing room of the colonial building housing the funeral home. They had come from all over. Some from as nearby as her dorm on campus, and some of those clothed in African attires arrived two nights before from Kenya, Malawi, and Gabon, her country. The coffin was white, just as she had wanted it, and her music of choice by Miriam Makeba was wailing quietly in the background. I looked around. All our teachers from campus were there. So were all members of the African community in the small university town nestled comfortably within the folds of the Appalachians, two hours away from bustling Columbus. Athens was witnessing its first funeral of a foreign student in decades, the students affairs officer informed a group of city people standing quietly by the little chapel in the home. I had not wanted to attend this viewing as I suspected it was going to be an emotional roller coaster for me, having seen her just a few days before she died. Some well meaning people—at least that was what they called themselves—had warned me just yesterday not to attend a funeral in my condition. You see, I am pregnant, and expected to put to bed anytime from now. The people, mostly members of our African community reminded me that it was a taboo anywhere in Africa for an expectant mother to wander around the same vicinity where a dead body is laid.

Don't you know that something bad may happen to this baby?
Aren't you concerned that her spirit may displace your baby?
What if you became ill of a mysterious illness?
Didn't you know what she died from?

And so on. I just listened as they talked, and thanked them when they were done. I didn't remind them that it was only less than a week ago that I stopped going to the hospital to see Hansa. That it was only because my baby threatened to come prematurely, and but for the doctor's dire warning that I should get an uninterrupted bed rest, I would have been there with Hansa the very day she died.

A woman had just screamed, and her screeching wail perforated the solemn façade of the gathering. The thrashing being was being helped up to her feet by her fellow Africans, comforting her in different languages. I recognized the grieving spectacle as one of Hansa's childhood friends who flew in that morning from her UN assignment in the Gambia. Her carefully coiffured hair hung limply around her grief swollen face. Some of the people that visited my house the day before were promptly by the woman and probably encouraging her to get a grip of herself. Or, maybe they were by now truly moved and were genuinely saddened by the whole thing. The Africans in the crowd were ululating loudly, not caring who was watching. Some were beating their feet to a rhythm only they could hear. Some of the men were grunting, as if in response to some unheard questions. Still others were just sitting with a faraway look in their eyes. Stunned as if they had just received the news. Hands grabbed collars. Hands pulled at carefully made hairdos. Hands ripped shirts. Hands cradled heads. Or merely held own neck in a choking fold. Some of the Americans seemed a little uneasy at the unabashed display of grief. One woman went and joined a group that was discussing the on-going coalition war in the Gulf. The man in front of me did not bother to look at the body inside the open casket, but merely lowered his gaze, made the sign of the cross, muttered something and tiptoed away from the scene.

The morticians sure performed some magic because the body inside the rectangular box had retained the healthy chocolate hue that glistened Hansa's skin when she was alive. It was nothing like what I saw just under a week ago when I last visited her. Then, her whole skin had been ravaged to a sickening pale pine. The hair had lost its shine, but look at it now; the magicians had replaced the ghostly worn out strands with shining braids that reached up to her long graceful neck. That same neck had been one edifice of skin badly bleached by assorted medication, with several lumps dancing along its scarred surface. Her face. That seemed to be the only body part that had not been tampered with. In its sleepy pose, it still retained a peaceful and comforting aura that made its owner appear as if she were merely resting in her favorite loft bed.

The more I viewed the remnants of what once held the vibrant soul of my friend, the more I was convinced that life must not cease following one's decease. I looked again and I thought I saw her eyes move. Her long arms were no longer flat and bony. They had injected some fluid inside her to make her appear so lifelike. She was dressed in her favorite African outfit, the two-piece up and down red and green skirt suit was a gift from her boyfriend.

Somebody sneezed behind me, and a chorus of voices wished the sneezer well. Heady perfumes wafted from all around, including from the casket. A profusion of fragrances hit my face, fragrances composed of citrus, vanilla, and some undistinguishable strong one that stung the nostrils and left a tangy taste in one's mouth.

When she was alive, Hansa attended the Catholic church in town; so I was not surprised to see the priest from her church among those waiting patiently behind me. I didn't know what to say to a dead body whose living replica I talked to just few days before. I memorized her peaceful pose, and moved away from the viewing space. Makeba was still lamenting a mother's loss in plaintive clicks as I meandered my way through the stinging fumes of cigarette smoke, past people waiting to use the restroom, past the smiling usher who wondered why I did not sign the visitors' book, into the welcoming fresh air.

Outside, I saw more people who had come to pay their respects, including her adviser, the friendly professor of cellular biology, the field in which Hansa was hoping to do her doctorate program. The lady came over to me, and embraced my willing body in a big hug. In between wiping her eyes and patting my back, she encouraged me to live the life Hansa would never experience.

Live her life for her. Okay? She will not like you to be unhappy. She really loved you. You girls were great friends. That doesn't have to end with her passing. Okay? You now must excel at your program . . . And so on.

As I walked slowly to my apartment, I avoided the enquiring gazes of students who had known me to be one of Hansa's most bereaved friends. I wanted to go back to my room and recollect Hansa. How could anyone live someone else's life for her, when one's own life is one long kaleidoscope. How else can one's life continue without a being to stretch that experience beyond the present? What kind of life would I be asking someone to live for me when I already have come to the end of my conscious one? Confusions galore. I resolved to think no more of Hansa, of death, of her illness, my own pregnancy. I just wanted to lose consciousness for a while. That was when I wished I drank. The last alcohol I touched was at my wedding reception several years ago, back in Nigeria, my own country.

Back in my apartment, I listened to my doctor's message on my answering machine informing me that I must report at his office as a lab report just arrived at his mail that afternoon. Two days ago, the good guy had ordered some additional test to verify the status of my baby. I missed his appointment already as he wanted me to come immediately. That was three hours ago. I decided nothing could be as urgent as Hansa in that white casket. Any other thing could wait. I went to bed thinking of my two boys attending a conference with their father in Hartford, and thanked the Supreme Being that I didn't have to worry about them for another two days. In my dream, the younger son called me on the phone, and asked if I was taking him and his brother to see Aunt Hassie. That's what they both called her. Hassie. I knew he meant if I was going to let them come to the hospital with me, so I told him that I would once auntie got better. The scene changed to a seaside that looked like one of those ocean resorts in Maryland. There we were. Hansa was playing soccer with the boys dressed in the same skirt attire she had on inside the white casket. I wanted to lure the boys away from her since I knew she was dead. But she kept throwing the ball at the boys, who ignored my calls and gleefully kicked the cotton-wool ball back. Every time they threw the ball, it floated softly over my body reclined on a beach chaise, and just before landing on my tummy, was gracefully reclaimed by a Hansa who by now had turned into an angel with Bob Marley braids.

Tell them about me. . . . 'bout me . . . Mommie, can we go home with Auntie Hassie . . . tell the boys about me. . . . Mommie come on, you pwomise..come on . . . The ball floated out of Hansa's hands and was hurtling through a clear blue sky toward my tummy. I dodged it and woke up with my hands out as if swiping at some fly.

I knew upon waking that I must write all I could recollect about Hansa. I also knew I was not going to let anyone know about my motivation to write the story. I resolved not to let anyone see the manuscript until it was safely in some publisher's good desk. My baby is due anytime now, so I really need to release the images stored in my mind before they all disappear into the caverns of forgetfulness. I decided to address the narrative to my unborn baby, as Hansa had wanted so much to be an active part of its life. Yes, its; because as a true African, I don't believe in knowing the gender of any pregnancy I'm carrying. The previous three had been nice surprises as my husband and I had warned our doctor during ultrasounds, against any unwanted revelation.

It all started a year ago.

You see, your aunt was not actually a blood relation. She was a friend that I met during my graduate days. She was reading for her Masters and I was into my second year of the doctorate program. I will tell you what these terms mean when you grow up. Your older brothers started calling her 'Antee' whenever she came over to our apartment. Where we presently live is set aside for married students and we've been here for close to six years now. Anti Hansa came into our lives in the third year of living here. She looked after Danjuma and Bade when I was expecting Ireti. She would come to the apartment after school every weekend to play soccer with your brothers. Then Danjuma was four years old, and Bade a feisty two and –a-half. I was up to my heels with class work. Looking back now, I must confess that I didn't mind all the studies I had to do then as they provided the break I needed from cleaning at the apartment. I was seven months pregnant with two younger kids and a husband who literally spent hours in his research lab which meant I had to sometimes wait until your brothers fell asleep before I could do anything relating to school. That was how when

Anti Hansa came and offered to keep me company at the apartment; it was like a god-sent.

She would take Dan and Bade out for about three hours at a stretch, sometime to her apartment downtown, but most of the times, it was to different places with interesting and fun spots for children. She once drove to Columbus with your brothers to show them a real city. Yes, the university was in a very sleepy town with little distraction for kids. It was and probably still is, a very serious environment for children. Now they have some more ice-cream places, and one or two more pizza joints. But at that time, the only fun venue for parents to take their children was the Play Place at the newly opened McDonalds.

So, it was a welcome relief to have Hansa come every weekend to play with your brothers, or just stay in the apartment helping me with cleaning and cooking. Your dad knew a lot of people and often invited fellow grad students, professors and visiting Africans to our townhouse apartment on campus. Hansa helped a lot in those times too. She would generally leave on Sunday evening after she'd made sure that I had all the main dishes I needed for the week. She prepared her favorite native dessert—rice pudding. This is just sticky rice boiled to a very soft consistency then mashed and mixed with coconut milk, sugar and vanilla. Your brothers gorged on this stuff, and you can see they still love rice pudding even now.

Anti Hansa came to the apartment one weekend, and on Sunday morning, just when she was preparing the tasty pudding, my water broke. Yes, that meant that Ireti was getting ready to come into this world. The night before, she and I had told the boys about where babies stayed until they were ready to come into the world. I remember Dan asking all the questions, and Hansa demonstrating her smart answers with dramatic gestures. I was unusually very restless, and Hansa advised that I went and lay down on the sofa that she had brought in from her apartment a week earlier on the complaint that it was too soft. I lowered myself on the flowery cushion and listened as Hansa and the boys engaged in a Question and Answer session about what babies did before coming to their mommies and daddies.

"Dan, let me tell you how . . ."

"Where was I before Mom had me?"

"Five years ago, you were right by the foot of the Great One"

"Who gweat one?"

"Bade, that's the same God, you know"

"Like they told us in Sunday school?"

"Yes, Dan. The same guy. Well, you were there one day,"

"By his foot?"

"Yes. And you looked down"

"Where I?"

"Bade, you were in one big room with other boys and girls"

"So, what happened, Anti?"

"If you would stop asking too many questions"

"Wharapen, Hansee?"

"Dan saw your mommie. And the Great One, the same Sunday school guy, well, he asked Dan if he would want to live with that fine lady down there"

"Uh-oh!"

"What Bade?"

"'Tee Hansee said the bad word. The bad word"

"Come on Bad, down there is not a bad word. H–E-double stick is"

"What are they saying, Titi"?

I waved my hand to indicate Hansa should disregard the interruption.

"You were in this golden palace with the Great One. You looked down past the clear blue skies, and your mom appeared. Several other women marched past and you pointed at your mom. The Great One asked if you would like to go there and live at her house"

"What Dan said?"

"I didn't say anything. I don't remember sitting at someone's feet. When did this happen?"

Their voices droned on as I drifted off only to be rudely awakened by a gush of very warm fluid bursting from between my legs.

The next hour was a blurry recollection of a calm Hansa packing up what she guessed I would be needing at the maternity ward in the next few days, while your excited dad called the doctor. She assured me that she would stay with the boys in the apartment while your dad went with me to the hospital. I did not argue but wobbled into her car. The trip to the hospital seemed to drag on and on. Finally, we arrived at the hospital and few minutes later, Hansa rushed back to her car so she could collect the boys from our next door neighbor.

They prepped me up at the hospital and prepared me for delivery. Only there was nothing happening. I was in labor for half–day and only opened up a miserly two centimeter. Now, that's a technical term that means the passage from where your head is to come out is only small enough to let out a tiny finger. When your aunt came around half past seven to find out what was happening, your dad informed her of the new development. He explained that since sixteen hours had lapsed and the passage was still just small enough for a baby's fist, the delivery team had decided to alert the surgeon who had come in promptly, took one look at the Xray that was taken during those painful hours and instantly ordered a C-section. He explained to me that the baby was presenting a difficult position called breach. That means your brother was not ready to come out of my tummy rolling on his head, like most babies.

"This fella is kneeling, Girl. You have a preacher there", the surgeon joked as he went into a room where two nurses began dressing him up in different garb–face mask, gloves, cap, even his shoes were covered with fluffy ones that almost looked like the winter floppies favored by your brothers. The only difference is the doctor's shoes had no droopy ears like Dan's rabbit's or paws like Bade's yellow flops.

They put me on drips as they wheeled me to the room where the operation would take place. By this time, I remembered having asked the nurses for something to relieve the raw pain around my waist. I was later told that I had asked for cocaine. You don't want to know what that is. I simply don't remember being that careless as to ask for something as bad as that thing. No, don't ask me what it is. Know for now that it is a very bad stuff that makes people do crazy things. Anyhow, I was telling you about the room where they wheeled me in. Inside was light blue. In the center was a bed, on which I was lifted. Your dad, in similar surgical garb as the doctor was by my right side. Make that right next to the right side of my head. I couldn't see him as the bright lights above me on the ceiling were almost blinding. Even if I wanted, I couldn't move my head as some contraption was holding it firmly to the white pillow. A voice floating at the back of my head slowly explained what would soon happen in the room.

You will be very conscious of everything in this room. You will see, hear and feel sounds. The doctor and his attendants are about to deliver your baby by cutting laterally through your abdominal wall, just above your pubic bone

As he droned on my eyes seemed to jump out of my face, leapt on the blue sheet that formed an artificial divider between my part of the room which started from where the gas doctor stood down to my breasts and two limp arms and hands crisscrossed with syringe tubes.

You will feel the weight of elephants walking on your tummy. .Now

don't fight it. It's just instruments spreading apart the thick wall of muscle in your abdomen as the doctor cuts through your uterus. That's a girl. Don't fight it. Just relax. . . . Good girl. Relax . . . Yeah . . . like that.

As if I could have done anything other than watch through eyes perched on the edge of the divider as gloved hands passed one instrument after the other from the tray on the foot of my bed to the surgeon whose cap I could only see.

The pressure was like nothing I'd ever experienced in all my life. It was just as the sleepy voice had predicted. It felt as if tons of bricks were lowered by unseen hands onto the spot above my navel. Owwhh!!! It was unbelievable. There is a book with the title about the unbearable lightness of being. At that moment in the delivery room, I wondered how lightness could ever be unbearable. That writer has not experienced the real heaviness involved in the process of bringing a being to life. Two pachyderm feet appeared in the space between the doctor's cap and the sheet separating my compartment. One heavy foot gently touched my body. Incredible pressure! I waited for the crack I knew must follow. I felt the whole of my chest cave in as the second foot kicked the first midair.

That's it. Don't fight it. You're doing good—

Laughter. Echoing guffaws. My chest reverberated with sounds. Flashing lights. Stifling pressure—Laughter disappearing, then suddenly resonating with unbearable clarity. Each time they laughed, I saw their laughter transformed in my imaginary screen into kaleidoscope of shapes—angular ones, geometric ones dancing in concentric colors that were a mixture of blue and steel. The shapes pulsated around the room as their voices traveled in and out of their mouths. Soon the elephants finished their parade on my body. The reverberating laughter and shapes disappeared, and the bouncing eyes focused on the new image that had displaced the colorful images. A baby wrapped in some blue blanket floated above the sheet. I knew that was your brother, Ireti. I was told that once they ripped him from my uterus, they lifted Ireti up and showed him to me. But I could not remember all that. What mattered then was knowing that the baby had ten of ten, two of two, his toes were not joined together, neither was his forehead flat. I saw his face under the funny cap and knew without fear that he was as normal as babies come. The doctor was wrong.

You see, I was told that I risked having an 'abnormal' baby because I had become pregnant with Ireti after my thirty-fifth birthday. Hmn-hmn. The doctor took one look at me that day on my first prenatal visit and predicted that your brother was going to be born with so many vital mental incapabilities. I immediately pictured Ireti with mongoloid eyes—droopy and always teary. The head in my scared mind's eyes was one contraption with thick skin, a creased forehead and a small nose dotted above a mouth out of which a thick tongue was sticking, unsuccessfully covered by thick drooling lips.

This same doctor also told me that your brother's feet on the ultrasound confirmed some abnormal chromosomes that fuse toes into an unrecognizable stump. With Dan, I had just one blood test, but since they suspected Ireti might not be a normal baby, the clinic ordered up to seven tests from four different blood draws.

Well, to cut a long story short, ten months later, they showed me a normal baby and I was so relieved I fell asleep.

When I woke up, Hansa was in the room. She had just come from the nursery and was ooh-ing and aah-ing about what a beautiful baby Ireti was. She had come with your older brothers. Bade didn't look that happy. Hansa explained that he had that sad face on because he had not been allowed to hold his new brother. I rang for the nurse and they explained to the boys that the pediatrician was busy taking the baby's vitals, and would not allow anyone to touch the baby. They came the next day, which was also the first time they got to hold Ireti in their arms. Dan was rather unsure of his ability to hold anything other than his favorite toy; as for Bade, he held the baby for as long as the duration of their thirty-minute visit.

The next day, the morning nurse came and told me that after lunch, I could call for a ride back to the apartment. I wondered if anything terribly important was happening on campus that required the presence of someone who just went under the knife few hours ago. The nurse looked blank for a second, and perking up immediately, explained in a deliberately slow voice that the hospital had assured me that I could leave for home forty-eight hours after the operation. I told her she should check the records by the foot of the bed: I had the baby by c-section just over twenty-nine hours ago. The on-call doctor came to my bed along with some resident doctors. He explained that I looked healed enough to go home. There and then I replied that what I was feeling was quite contrary to his description, and that, yes indeed, I too was up to date with the new laws that required women who had just undergone C-section to be allowed to stay in hospital care for at least forty-eight hours.

I tried to be calm, and not angry especially knowing that with this baby, my husband and I had a respectable carrier for our health insurance purposes. I didn't want to think that the staff was ignorantly assuming that I was a poor minority woman who probably was on welfare. I wanted to scream at them all, but I remembered what my mother once said about new mothers. They were not to consciously entertain negative attitudes following births, since energies from the land of the unborn had not been completely detached. She told me that mothers had to wait for seven days in case of a boy, and eight if it's a girl before letting all her consternation out. I had six more days to accommodate these fools, so instead of cursing them in Yoruba, I gently explained that aside from all the reasons I had already given, I was still feeling very sore around my waist where a bead of staples had been used to clamp shut the obstetric gash. Moreover, I needed strength to carry the baby around, which I presently couldn't do. The retinue around my bed looked relieved when the door opened and my real doctor came in. He advised the staff to leave me alone until I was strong enough to go home.

We were discharged four days later. Enough time to have Ireti circumcised. Twice as long the time regular insurance would have sanctioned the extended stay. Thanks to my understanding doctor, at the end of a week-stay at the hospital, I felt very refreshed and had just one extra week to remove the staples around my waist.

Hansa came for us that day, three years ago, because your dad had to lead an experiment at the lab to some visiting high school kids. She stayed at the apartment until I had those pins removed from the surgical site on my abdomen.

Then Hansa fell ill.

The first time your aunt was ill was the day before Ireti's first birthday. She shared a two-bedroom apartment downtown with another graduate from Maine. Heidi was a flamboyant fine arts major who was as nice as Hansa but much less visible. She traveled a lot with the theater company, and when she was not performing meditated inside her room humming like traumatized bees. I saw Heidi maybe three times altogether. So, when Hansa fell ill, I didn't know because her roommate did not tell me. She had traveled with the university troupe to Scotland on a two-week trip. Anyhow, I noticed that Hansa was absent at the class we both registered for. I should tell you about Hansa's love for literature. She once told me that it was tough deciding what to major in when she first matriculated at her country's premier university. She had been an all-A student at the A-Level examination; however, the knowledge that her country paid more scholarship money for science related courses than the humanities, made her ditch English for Biology. When she arrived in Athens for her graduate programs, she didn't think she would have the opportunity to study literature even as an elective. After all, what relationship did one have with the other. In the end, she found that two courses from the humanities would only enhance her liberal education. So she registered in and excelled at one course that I particularly did not like. Transformational grammar for me was too complicated; but Hansa breezed through and helped me with the boring assignments. The other class that she registered in happened to be one of her favorites. Twentieth Century Literature was also my neck of the wood, and we usually met after class, so it was unusual when I didn't see her in two class meetings. She was scheduled to present a paper on Virginia Woolf's *Mrs Dalloway*, but she was not in class.

I called her apartment. No answer. Then I went there only to be told by the lady who lived upstairs that the 911 people came for Hansa that very morning, and yes, I could go check the hospital. She wasn't sure if they had taken her there, or the one in Columbus, a good two-hour trip.

They didn't allow me to see her at first at the hospital. I explained to the chatting nurses in their flowers and butterflies uniforms that I need to see Hansa. Why? They wanted to know.

"Because I am her friend."

"What's your name?"

I told them.

For good three minutes, two nurses shuffled through sheets of papers stacked inside a yellow folder.

"What's your name again?"

I stuck out my driver's license. The overweight aide studied the picture in the card; looked at my frowning face, decided it was the same face even though the picture was taken a year after I had your oldest brother. Then I was at least ten pounds lighter, did not wear braids, and probably had a much cheery face than now. She handed back the license. I snatched it, much to my own annoyance; I didn't want to lose my temper.

"So, can I go see her?"

"That depends on what her boyfriend says."

I slumped in the chair. Just then the other nurse rushed out of a room several yards from the nurses' station.

"Yes, she can. Her name is among those okayed She's one of her friends. Make sure you have her name in for future visits."

I followed the corpulent aide to Room 210B.

There were two other nurses by the door when we got there. One of them asked me to cover my face with a face mask that she pulled out from a stack by the wall, over which was written 'hazardous'. I hesitated, questions spilling all over my face.

"Oh, it's for your friend's protection . . ."

"Her name is Hansa"

"Well, whatever . . . She's in a very vulnerable condition now to the extent that an innocent sneeze from any one of us can kill her."

I put on the mask. The other nurse tied the knot behind my head. It was difficult to breathe into the foil nose guard. The thing smelled like stale plastic bag sprayed with some fungicidal powder. With the mask securely tied to my face, the guards at the door motioned me in. I entered Room 210B.

And I saw her.

Hansa was flat on her back in a hospital bed that had been hoisted up to a comfortable recline for her. Pillows supported her braided head, and her arms were resting on the padded cushion by each side of her bed. Her slim long frame was covered with a white bed sheet. She looked sleepy, beads of sweat plastering the disheveled braids all over her face. Everything was quiet inside the room; except those machines. There was one behind her head that held hoses and contraptions responsible for her breathing. The noise reminded me of bubbles fish make while swimming inside a small aquarium .

The door opened. A nurse tiptoed in and informed me that I had to leave. That my five minutes were up. I just got here! I screamed in my head.

"Five minutes?" I asked.

"No more. Just five minutes ma'am. You can come again tomorrow."

Your Anti Hansa was still rather sleepy when I left that room.

I went back the next day and was allowed to stay for twenty minutes. Still Hansa lay sleeping. The artificial breather was there too. When I returned the third day, the breathing machine had been turned off. Her own breath came in irregular puffs. Her boyfriend left the room just as I walked in. Hansa was sitting up in the chair by her bedside. I knelt beside her there and she held my hand. Her hands were very warm, but stable. No shaking or grasping; they felt restive in my palm. We didn't say anything until she indicated she needed to use the bathroom. I reached for the ringer by her bed, but she wouldn't have it that way. Leaning her almost six feet frame on my shoulder, she made it to the bathroom a mere five feet from her bed. I helped her back on the bed still wondering what ailed her.

"Is it Flu?"

She smiled and started coughing. She spat in a cup covered with a plastic lid. When the fit subsided, I wiped her mouth. She lowered her head on the fluffy pillow. Then she shook her head.

"No, it'sh not the flu."

Her words sounded funny. She had lost some weight and whenever she talked her teeth appeared bigger than they really were. Her folder was by the foot of her bed, and I resolved to catch a glimpse of the diagnosis. She asked about your brothers, whom she called her team. Now the word sounded like 'theme' She used to play soccer with them months before she fell ill. I told her they too missed her and it was then I remembered the card your brothers had signed in their hen-pecked handwriting. She picked out the picture of the boys from the envelope and motioned to the window where three pots of flowers sat. I placed the picture of four year-old Dan and almost three years Bade in a bathtub right in the middle vase, a beautiful basket of African violets.

"Jreamt I was danshing"

"Dancing?" I asked quietly covering the patient folder which I had stealthily opened while placing the picture.

She was breathing rather harshly. I wished she could stop talking. I told her so. She shook her head and smiled as she repeated her latest dream

"I was-sh danshing with some sk- sh-kelet- shkeletons"

We were both quite superstitious even though we came from two different cultures. She once told me several months before, after our common course of a dream in which she had lost all of her teeth. I remembered telling her in a playful manner that hid the trepidation of the supposed ominous outcome that that was usually a bad dream. You see, as a child, my mother told me that if I dreamt that I lost my teeth, then I was headed for a serious illness. When Hansa first told me of her teeth motif dream, I remembered how my sister would always dream of lost teeth. Hers. Not any other person's. She never told my mother of her recurrent dream as she was conscious of the supposed interpretation. Serious illness. Probability of death. Definitely ominous.

"I was dansh—dancing with two ske-skeletons, Titi." Hansa whispered again, and a tear rolled down the corner of her sallow eyes. I wiped the tear off her drained face and reassured her

"Don't worry, Love, you'll be fine."

"Three shkeletons"

I thought she said two. What's the use. Two or three, it's still dead bones

"Titi. That'sh not good. Baad"

I felt her fear. I wiped her face again with a Kleenex from her bedside drawer. "Don't worry Dear, you'll be fine."

I desperately wanted to believe that, but my fear rolled down with another teardrop. I wiped her face. The door opened and the nurse came in with Hansa's boyfriend in tow.

I didn't wait for the nurse to shoo me out. I simply kissed Hansa lightly on her warm cheek and tasted the wet saltiness of her tears. She was already sleeping as I walked to the door.

"What exactly is wrong with her?" I asked the nurse outside the room.

She said something about talking to the doctor. That she didn't really know. I found that so strange that a nurse would come into a patient's room, administer certain medication, read her charts and still claim ignorance of her condition. I ruled David out as he resented the fact that Hansa demanded that my name be included on the list of special guests. He knew I too resented the notion of him not including me in the very first instance.

Hansa stayed at the hospital for three more days, and I visited her every one of those days. When I returned on the last day of her first stay at the hospital, Hansa was looking much like her ebullient self. Her slightly stooped gait had straightened She talked without aspirating her letters. She could walk by herself. When I got to her room, she had made up her bed and had her bag packed in readiness for the doctor's dismissal. I knew her boyfriend was coming to get her but she told me that she would love to fully recuperate at my apartment. She didn't want to go to David's place because it was rather noisy there. I encouraged her to choose my place because she would need special African soups only three of us on campus knew how to make. The only other person was an American professor who did her peace corps program in Gambia where she mastered the art of preparing groundnut soup in the two years she lived in that central African country . She made the best groundnut soup. I remember that day that Hansa was very happy and reminded me to prepare her favorite jollof rice, rice pudding and pepper soup.

I had those food items warming in the oven before I went to see her, with the confidence that she was coming to my house to recover from whatever she had just gone through at the hospital. I remember that morning as we both waited for the doctor to discharge her, Hansa took my hand and said in a clear voice

"I had that dream again, Titi."

Even though I knew what she meant, I feigned ignorance.

"Oh what dream?"

"You know—the one with the skeletons."

"Oh—"

"And you know what? There were five of them yesterday."

"Five?" I wanted to lighten the heavy effect

"Yes. Five." She held up her hands, and her long fingers unfolded like delicate tendrils. "Five."

"Well—What music were you dancing to?"

"Can you believe it?—Waltz! We were waltzing all over this long hallway!"

"Come on Hansa, that's just the five weekdays you spent in this boring room."

I hugged her.

"Or—it probably means in five weeks, months, or—"

"Shushhhh—Baby. You are tired and should get out of this room before you add the doctor himself to your dancing list."

"No, Titi, only five possible dancers because you see, they each came out of a room along the hallway—"

"Hansa! I'll see you later."

"Tell the boys I'll see them soon."

I got a call from David two hours after I left Hansa's room at the hospital that she was going to be in his apartment. No, not just for one day; but until she was strong enough to take care of herself. I didn't want to interfere, especially after my husband advised that I should back off. He reminded me that David needed to feel useful, and my constant presence in Hansa's life following her discharge might be wrongly construed. I frankly didn't see the direction of the advice; I only suspected that he must have sensed some misgivings from David's friends and he didn't want my good intentions to be insulted. Other people came and reminded me that I had enough responsibilities to choke my twenty-four hours a day existence. There were two toddlers and a baby, along with freshman courses to teach and a comprehensive exam to prepare for. They advised that I kept off worrying about Hansa for two weeks, enough time to allow David to prove he could take proper care of Hansa. I reluctantly agreed and told David to let me know of Hansa's daily development. He left a message on my answering machine that he would call me at the end of every week, not every day as I had requested.

I traveled to New Orleans for a conference, and by the time I came back, I was burning with eagerness for news about my friend. I asked my husband if David had called about Hansa. He said no.

I called David's apartment. No one picked the phone. I went there but the door to his room was locked. People assured me they had seen David around the campus, but without Hansa. I went to the department to inquire if she had attended class during my absence. The secretary did not recollect seeing Hansa throughout that week. By this time I was so scared. Did she travel? I called David's apartment at least three times, leaving messages after each call.

Back in my apartment, I threw away all the fresh produce I had bought each farmers' market day. Hansa loved fresh salad made from the array of healthy spread. I finally convinced myself that she had traveled home to Gabon to see her mother, just as she had wanted to since the previous summer.

Few days later, in the class that I took with Hansa, someone said she saw David in one of the dorms in the Green. I asked myself how could that be, since David would not go near student dorms, as he once told Hansa that any building with young university students reminded him of his undergraduate days back in his East African country where some of his friends who were student activists were brutally shot by the military police during students' demonstration against certain corrupt leaders.

When the student in my Literature class saw the puzzled look on my face, she informed me that David was the new Assistant Director of her dorm, along with "her sick friend."

"Hansa?"

"Yes. They said she is in the other dorm."

I drove to the dorm indicated. I knew that Hansa was to have assumed duties as the RD of that Hall, following her discharge from the hospital, but the whole excitement surrounding her illness obliterated that from my mind.

I knocked on the door.

No reply.

I wished the doors here had keyholes through which one could peep, like back home in Nigeria. At least I would be able to tell if she was there or not. I was that desperate.

I called David's room.

No reply.

I called Hansa's room.

The same thing. No response.

On the third day after the discovery of her new residence, I decided to get to the bottom of Hansa's real whereabout. I called her room very early that day, around five in the morning. That was the kind of time only serious calls would be made by those of us from outside the US. That was also when we usually received calls from our relatives.

Predictably, David picked up the phone.

"Hello?"

"Yes–It's me, Titi."

"Oh—"

"Oh—? That's all you can say? Where is Hansa?"

"She's here."

"Oh—? Here? You mean in that room? Since when?"

The phone clicked.

"Hello—Hello—David?"

No answer. The dial tone confirmed he had disconnected the call.

My first class that day was from eleven to one in the afternoon. I left the apartment with the boys in their father's care, and headed for Hansa's new apartment. I saw her car parked in the space marked 'RD'. I'd seen David drive that car several times. I parked my Nova beside the white Ford Taurus. Her country's flag swirled on a flagpole mounted in the backseat.

I climbed the six stairs to the third floor and right in front of her door was David, book bag slung on his shoulder, about to lock the door.

"Where is she?"

He dropped his bag

"Why didn't you call before coming?"

I pushed the door open. Then I saw her.

"I'm sorry Titi. I know how you will take this, but please, know that I tried my best, my very best, to get her back to the hospital, but she won't leave her room—You know what she is like once her mind is made up—"

I saw Hansa.

She was longer than the bed on which she lay stretched out like a carefully packed sack of bones covered in a sleeping robe. Her arms, much longer than I'd ever seen on anyone, not even on tall ones like her, showed another feature. A strange and frightening feature. The arms were flat. Flat like thin planks of pine chiseled into femur and tibia and Edward Scissorshand fingers.

She said something in French.

"Hansa—it's me. Titi"

Tears burned my cheeks as they dropped in continuous drip. I flopped to my knees. David had closed the door behind me and was in the room. I turned in his direction, and he left the room as he read my face.

"Hansa, what happened to you?"

There were two holes two inches deep in her face where two bright eyes glazed feverishly. Another hole between her ear and her head pulsated dangerously.

She said something in her native language.

"Come on Hansa. It's me. I don't speak Myene. It's Titi . . . Ti—ti. Yes, Me." I kept whispering in whimpers taking in all her emaciated limbs, sunken glowing orbs and stringy shaggy hair.

Cancer! It came to me as if in a trance. It must be cancer. They told me in those awful weeks after my sister's death, when Hansa came to help me with the kids, that my sister on her death bed looked like a sack of bones. She must have looked exactly like Hansa that day I found her in her room, a mere half-a-mile away from my own apartment, locked away from prying eyes of concerned friends, by her boyfriend who could not get her out, because he could not break his promise to her not to reveal the nature of her ailment.

Two drawn eyes flicker–"Tthh—Tiii"

I knew then that she recognized me. The two orbs clouded with mist. I looked on, paralyzed with anger, with profound sadness.

The door opened. The boyfriend came in, touched my shoulder and whispered that I must leave, as Hansa was getting tired.

I slowly rose to my feet, but dropped back down as my hands were still locked in Hansa's grip. I was astonished at the strength. I looked at her again. There she was; two holes in a face slowly oozing tears into ears that shone with an unhealthy glow. Long lashes gummed shut even as tiny balls stretched their rubbery transparent lids. The grip softened as her hands lay limp by her side.

I slid out my hands and asked the boyfriend why she was breathing so harshly. The space where two breasts once stood so proudly now resembled a campsite rudely evacuated. I could not see where they sagged on her emaciated body.

With my sister I remembered being informed that on her deathbed, her whole chest seemed to have caved in, leaving a huge dent in the stomach area. But then, I reasoned, not eating anything for days could result in such flattened spectacle.

"Come on Titi, you really have to leave."

"Alright! But just tell me what you are going to do about her. How long has she been like this? Why didn't you take her to the hospital? Do you see her skin coloration? Does that look normal to you?"

Maybe he attempted some self-curative experiments on her. Like what abortion would mean; so much blood loss. But yanking a baby from anybody's uterus could not have left the victim this colorless, this eaten up, this ravaged, this. . . .

I was literally dragged out of the room, but not before flashing David my most accusative look that screamed defiantly at his angry face, which at that moment stared back with such irritation as one saw on Voodoo priests who'd been cheated by ungrateful clients.

"Will you at least tell me what is wrong with her!" I screamed behind the door.

With shaky legs, I wobbled three floors down to the car park. My head swooned. My face burned. Things made noise in my ears. I sat down for a long time in the car waiting for the emotions to subside.

Back home, I fed the boys and relieved their father who had missed a class while awaiting my return from the Greens. He knew something bad had happened, or was happening, or, was about to happen. Knowing me, however, he didn't bother asking since I wouldn't have been coherent in that state of mind. The boys had to be taken to the Park. We whiled away two hours, after which all three grew tired and started whining in different manners. The oldest began pushing an empty swing. The middle boy proceeded to throw sand at the slide which led to angry parents shaking multicolored fingers at the pudgy toddler.

Once home, I prepared for next-day activities. I signed pre-school notice found in the three year-old bag. I looked over the Tiger Cubs schedule and was relieved to find there was no den meeting until the following week. My mind raced ahead of sensible considerations. What if she died? What would happen to her body? Did she think of death? Oh my Gosh—I hope nothing bad happens to Hansa. Help me oh God.

"Mom!"

"Mom!"

"Mooommm!! It's time for Ninja Turtles!" The three year-old pulled at my housecoat, and pointed at the TV set. I knew what he wanted.

"No, it's not! That doesn't show on weekdays. It's Saturday!!" The five year-old explained to his brother.

"It's okay, Dee. I know your brother wants to play one of your Ninja movies. Can you please put one on for him? Please?"

"But, Mom, I want to see *Home Alone*"

"Yes, you'll see that after he's watched *Ninja Turtles*. OK?"

The next three weeks were a flurry of graduate school events, family-based activities as determined by the number and ages of children in that particular household and seemingly endless visits to the local hospital where Hansa was rushed to the evening I discovered her locked up in her room. I remember calling the campus director of international office, and telling him all I could lucidly recount of what I saw in that residence hall. He immediately dispatched an ambulance and when I heard that they had removed my friend from her room, I was hugely relieved. At least, I was comforted that she would be under professional care.

She was in that hospital for two weeks, during which I had written and passed my comprehensive exam. I could not tell her that, because by then she could not talk, as that ability had joined the rest of her mental capacities on the artificial table. Her system packed up in stages. At first, it was her lungs that refused to properly purify the blood; so she was hooked onto an artificial breathing machine. Two days later, I saw the dialysis machine next to the array of tubes, hoses, canisters all around her bed. Then one day, I came in and saw a tube trailing from under her bed to some spot under her robe. The new contraption silently making whisking noise confirmed my suspicion; that the liver had failed too.

When I visited her the second day after her admission, we could talk, albeit she did in aspirated whispers. Her mood was very depressed. She suspected her boyfriend of cheating on her. Even though I didn't care for David, one thing I dared not question, because there was no visible evidence, was his total devotion to Hansa. So, I reassured her that she was imagining things. She was quiet for a while, and all I could hear was the whirling, hissing, and assorted sounds coming from the life support machine that was gradually reclaiming natural functions.

At the end of the second week, she was rushed into the intensive care unit. Apparently, her brain forgot to drain excess fluid from her cranium. When I arrived at the hospital that evening, no one was allowed in. I was asked to come back twelve hours later, after which she should have come out of danger. I forgot how that day went at home; I probably carried on my mom duties at home, and rushed to the ICU few hours later. This time, I was allowed in, and David was not there. Hansa's head was all swathed in wraps of white bandage. The head appeared much larger than normal, with the forehead protruding dangerously from under the swath. She was sleeping, and I could only stay for five minutes. The ICU nurse informed me that they would transfer Hansa back to her room in two more days, and I was to visit only once she got back to her room. I took one more glance at my dear friend, and left.

I had to leave for my new job the very next day. I had arranged with my husband to come back home every day, even though the new school was located three hours away. There were two major reasons for the shuttling: my family and my friend. I needed to know what was happening at home with three young kids in care of their busy father, and Hansa's swollen head frightened me so much I knew I could not keep away longer than two days.

On the third week of her admission at the hospital I left for work as usual on a Monday morning, after spending much of Saturday with now totally-hooked–to-life supporting-machine Hansa. That Saturday, we were incommunicable, as our last attempt at communicating was before her head was bloated with whatever fluid the brain forgot to drain. On her part, Hansa exerted all her mental effort on sign language. We had gone from aspirated whispers to hand talk where one clutch by me meant I was leaving, and two jerky tugs at my finger meant I should stay until she fell asleep. That got a little confusing, because she would sometimes refuse to shut her eyes. Then there were the blinks. One meant she heard me. Half-open blinks indicated she was not sure, and a deliberate roll of the iris from right to left showed she was thinking about something. She had also got to refusing to close her lids. That meant she didn't want me to leave. I knew I wouldn't be able to visit her on Sunday, because my church would be organizing a potluck somewhere away from the campus. Knowing we would return from that potluck picnic late, well past the visiting hours at the hospital, when I left Hansa's room that weekend, I promised to return after I came back from work on Monday.

I had just finished teaching my second class that Monday morning when my head of department called me to her office. My ears rang bells, and my hands got sweaty. On my way to the lady's office, I recalled my dream of the night before. I saw Hansa crawling out from under a bed where she had been crushed, getting to her feet and stretching out with her hands wide open and her head thrown back in sheer relief.

"Hello"

"Oh . . . Titi?"

"Yes? . . . What is it?"

"It's Hansa"

"Yes..? Please, don't tell me"

"I'm sorry, Love. It was yesterday night . . . Titi . . . Are you there?"

"Err . . . Yes . . ."

That was a week ago. Now, everything seems so unreal. It's hard to believe she is really gone. On the other hand, I'm happy that she no longer has to endure pains, hallucinations and all those frightening mirages that haunted her last weeks.

As I get ready for my eighth pre-natal visit, I resolve to name the baby after Hansa, and probably write another memoir. But it won't be the same. Whatever it turns out to be, I know I'll be rest assured that I've fulfilled Hansa's injunction to tell my children about her. I hope, my dear baby, when you are out of my womb, and old enough to read, you will get to know and love your surrogate aunt, my dearest Hansa.

The Teasing Sunset

The first time I noticed the sun must have been three years before that after-noon in Ifo when I went with my cousin and my two sisters to the village farm two miles away from the family house we shared with our strict aunt.

Three years before that afternoon, I was a mere four year-old curious be-ing perched on top my father's shoulders watching the sun miraculously turn from a friendly fiery blinding ball to an overripe pawpaw sliced and draped in a perfect arch on the sky outside my father's work shed. He would take me from our house to that spot by his shed to watch the glorious sunset. I re-member three years before that afternoon at Ifo, that my father always ex-plained that the sun that we just saw change daylight into instant darkness was called *tonmodesoko*. When I asked why they named the sun such a rude name, my father had smiled and pointed at the sun which by then had all but disappeared into the hills beyond the work shed.

"See?" He pointed.

I couldn't see anything as the horizon above where the sun recently radi-ated its resplendent glory was all dark and twinkling with teasing stars.

Later that day, I asked my mother why people called the evening sun *ton-modesoko* . Like my father, she too had smiled but she explained

"The *tonmodesoko* is a messenger sent to warn errant children to go back home."

"But how will they find their way back home if it has turned dark on them?"

"The wise boy or girl would know because the sun would have lost its heat."

"Oh . . . ?"

At seven years old, I was a very bright, still curious girl in primary three. I had outgrown my father's shoulders and now living with my aunt, always looked forward to visiting him only on holidays. When we got back home that day from my father's work shed, he promised to take me to the village where he grew up; just so he could show me the most perfect *tonmodesoko*.

I remember it was just as eerie as the ones over his shed. Only this time, because there was nothing retracting the rays of the sun as there was no electric light in the whole village, the *tonmodesoko*'s grand exit was a real show. At first, it was all bright with those village boys playing soccer, kicking cans and empty gourds all over the school field; the next minute you heard mothers calling for their children, dogs barking and chickens being hurried into their coops. Back in the city, my father was transferred to another town and he sent me and my two sisters to live with his sister in the village until he and my mother sent for us.

I'd been in that ancestral village for three years when my aunt decided I was old enough to join my siblings and our cousin in doing after-school chores. Don't get me wrong, even at five years-old, I had my own little chore. I was the designated dishwasher. I washed what plates I could find stacked outside the kitchen door. What I couldn't finish washing I threw away—while no one was looking—far into the banana plantation behind the outhouse. I also picked up after my aunt. Overall, whatever I did before I turned seven, was done at home. However, upon reaching the age of reasoning, my aunt decided that I was old enough and ready to experience much more challenging chores.

On my own part, I was happy. Who liked to stay at home running endless errands between the outdoor kitchen and the house? Whatever needed fetching, I fetched it.

"Peju, go and fetch the gallon of oil-"

"Peju, where is the salt? -"

"Come on. Shell the melon seed"

"Go and fetch the lantern-"

"Has that cat just entered my room? Peju, go and get it out!"

And so on.

We always trooped in from school every afternoon at half-past two. On Thursdays, all four of us remembered to be present at the church hall for choir practice. And we made sure we got there on time too. Aside from having our aunt's uncle—my great-uncle—as the choirmaster, we had the added misfortune of a choirmaster who was a stricter person than our aunt. If you went in two minutes after the *tunic solfa*, you recited the Lord's Prayer seven times. In Yoruba and English. God help the latecomer if he/she happened to be a relative; in that case, the offending chorister was given two heavy knocks on the head. We all knew of our great-uncle's sternness, so took special care to always be among the early arrivals.

The day after our usual choir practice, my aunt sent us to the farm that was two miles away from the village. She had left for Lagos soon after we came back from school and had left word that we were to change from our school uniform into regular clothing, after which we were to have our rice and beans lunch, and then proceed to the farm.

"Girls, you are going to collect some firewood, gather some mushroom, pick some tangerines and head back before it turns dark-"

Olu, her daughter and our cousin was also the oldest. She was the wood fetcher, Ola and Tinu, my older sisters were the ones to pluck tangerines and my humble first chore outside my aunt's kitchen was to pick as many mushrooms as the swampy farm could provide. We knew that my aunt was not coming back from Lagos that day, as it was a Friday, and the last train to Lagos came Friday afternoon, and she would not get a return ride back until late on Saturday. We waved to our aunt as she quickened her pace to the railway station where she would board the Idogo train for Lagos.

We made the two-mile trip to the farm in a speedy fifty minutes. Guided by the bright sun, we arrived at the orchard where our ancestors first planted the tangerines, oranges, cashew, guava, along with the cocoa, coffee and kolanut trees. There were four of us ranging in age from fourteen to seven—me being the youngest. We remembered that we had various chores to do at the farm, but we also knew that we could finish the main chores before it got dark; or so we thought.

The only person that needed to do her chores elsewhere was Olu, our cousin whose assignment was to collect firewood. She told us she would do that later, since it was still bright and sunny; too warm to go inside some thorny bush for some stupid dried sticks and wood. She pulled my older sister Tinu, to another corner of the farm and soon, they were both testing who could throw which fruit the longer distance. They wanted to improve their skill at netball, they explained as they giggled each time a guava landed in the nearby stream, or a ripe cocoa burst its succulent beans all over the cassava patch. They seemed to be having a good time.

Under a tree not too far away from Olu and Tinu's netball practice, Ola, my immediate older sister hoisted me on her shoulder so I could reach the tempting bunch swaying with golden and light-green oranges. I reached out one strained arm, grabbed one of the branches, shook oranges all over the ground, surprising some bees that were comfortably sucking the nectar. I dodged my head trying to avoid the angry swarm, and simultaneously, one huge orange rolled over my back, hit Ola in the face, and she involuntarily dropped to the ground.

I felt air where Ola's shoulder had provided sure footing for my weight, and hugged the branch all the way to the ground. Relieved that we were not stung by the bees, Ola and I ran toward our older relatives and resumed our bee halted activity. The four of us played soccer with fallen tangerines, squashed cocoa pods, sucked the juicy pulp and spat out the beans. We repeated the process on ripe cashew fruits and assorted pawpaws. We kicked and scattered kolanut pods all over the farm.

It happened before we knew it. Olu was on top of the kolanut tree shaking off pods she was certain held more than the common two-lobed nuts. Tinu, the eleven year-old was by the vegetable bed, a few yards from the kolanut trees, while Ola and I were busy admiring the nearly foot-long millipede circling the mushroom shrub.

The *tonmodesoko* disappeared behind Tinu's head casting a sickly pinkish-bronze hue on the horizon. Then the bronze melted and got mixed with powdered charcoal making my sisters appear like ghosts with no heads. Soon, everything was black. Pitch black. The bright friendly sun turned our playground on the farm to the most frighteningly dark landscape. It was very confusing. Darkness crept on us at the same time the sun was warming our faces.

Four girls began whimpering.

"Yeh-eh, we are done for!" Olu shouted

"Hey, we're done for-"

"Ah—Auntie will kill us today"

"That is if the *agatus* didn't eat us before midnight"

"Ohhh—"

"Why—why didn't we do our chores before this stupid sunset catch us, ehn?"

"But whoever thought *Tonmodesoko* would leave for its home this early"

That from me who by now had become so scared that all I saw were moving trees, and flying beings. I thought I heard elephants trumpeting. I told them. More wailing.

"What are we going to do?"

"Nothing. Let's just trace our steps back to the village."

"How?"

Something slithered past my head. I screamed. Tinu hissed, assuring me it was just the rope she had cut earlier on; but there were no firewood pieces, nothing to use the rope for. I could not believe that the sun whose brightness cast dancing shadows on the cocoa tree could miraculously disappear. To worsen the whole problem, none of us had started her chore. We knew we were in big trouble.

"Ah . . . what shall we tell Mama?" Tinu wailed, twirling the rope.

I felt my way around the cocoa tree, searching for where my basket was. I could not find it. I started crying silently, scared of attracting the nocturnal attention of all the *iwins* and *oros* that my primary Two storyteller teacher told the class roamed the forest at night.

Sounds. Screeches. Strange birds. Gasps, muffled cries from four frightened girls all cuddled around the foot of the huge kolanut tree.

"What are we going to do?"

We could not see our baskets, lost perhaps in the forest, which I believed
now were teeming with beings walking on their heads. Or, the beings were
probably hiding or just playing with our baskets which few minutes earlier,
we had merrily kicked all over the farm.

We felt around for each other's hands, or arms; just anything to grasp. We
each felt a great urge to touch something, or someone to reassure ourselves
that we would be alright. Before I knew what was going on, I felt my arm almost yanked off my shoulder as Tinu dragged me toward the clearing, which
also was the path that we would take back home.

I smelt the river before we waded through. Olu was in front, followed by
Ola who was pulling on Olu's wet dress. I was behind Ola because they all
decided that being the youngest of the group, it would be proper for me to be
almost in the middle. Tinu held onto the belt on my dress, silently simpering.
For some strange reason, the river felt so wide that night. There was no moon-
light to help us through; the darkness was so thick we couldn't even see any
reflection in the water as we frighteningly rush through the seemingly endless
width. Olu had instructed all of us before we left the farm not to think of anything once we got to the river. There had been rumors of dead people floating
all over the riverbank, throwing stones and broken crab shells at passers-by.
We were to suspend our thoughts, and just pretend we were not crossing the
river. Well, I wanted so desperately to do all that, but my mind failed me, and
I started crying.

"Shut Up, Peju!"

"Leave her alone, Olu. Ah-ahh, as if you too are not afraid"

"Will you girls just shut up! Keep quiet!!"

"Tinu, who are you telling to shut up? Me? I'll show you respect when we
get home! You'll see!!"

"If we get home"

When Ola said this, I thought I saw something move to my left. My head
swelled, as if thousands of ants were crawling all over a bald pate. There
should be nothing but an old Iroko tree, but I was so sure I saw something
move. My head still felt as if I was wearing nothing but a basket of cotton
wool .So I broke loose, screaming and crashing into Ola in front of me. She
lost her grip on Olu who pelted the moment she heard me scream.

Four disheveled, screaming girls tore into the village alarming villagers
who were variously getting dinner ready, or supervising homework, or just
sitting in their front yards. We stopped right in front of the village chief's
house. We could not go further as the whole villagers had stopped whatever

they were doing and poured out of their hovels blocking our way. Someone ran to call our aunt, shouting "They are back! They are here!! Mama Olu, we found them!!"

Olu hissed when she heard the man say that. She spat out her disgust and grumbled under her breath, "Stupid man, nobody found us. Listen girls, we were almost kidnapped by the Agatus"

"What?"

"Shhh. You heard me. We are going to tell Mama that those Agatus tried to kidnap us."

"Bbb..But, they did not!"

"Sshhh, Peju; stupid girl. They did, because if we don't come up with something as serious as that."

"Sshhh, Olu, someone is coming."

"What's wrong with this girl? .Someone is coming indeed!! Aren't we surrounded by the whole village?"

"Stupid, it's Mama. She's coming..Yes, she's behind those women."

"Now, everyone, remember, it's the Agatus."

"But..our baskets. Won't they want to..?"

"Shhhut up Peju!!!"

Mama was flanked by a retinue of villagers who had apparently been consoling her on the loss of four children. She looked haggard and worn out. Her *gele* had come unloosened, forming a noose around her neck.. Her arms cradled her head, signifying total despair. Some of her best friends were holding onto her wrapper that threatened to come undone. Her uncle, our strict great uncle and choirmaster stepped forward. Some villagers floated to the other side of the road, leaving four girls in the middle of the road. The old man whispered something to my aunt. She heaved, sighed, rubbed her hands together, then opened them in the direction of the sky. From habit, I knew my aunt would do that anytime she was relieved about a near mishap. She lifted her face upwards again, while her uncle walked up and down in front of us, as if trying to study our faces.

"What happened? Hen? Olu, speak!"

"I. emm . . . we"

"Uncle, let Peju talk, she will tell the truth"

"No, Sir..I mean sir, we were . . . they"

"Olu said to. . . ."

"No, Sir . . . I'll tell you what happened"

"Uncle! Uncle!! I said don't let Olu or Ola talk. They lie. Ask the little girl"

"*Ngbo*, Peju, can you tell us what"

"It's the Agatus sir!!!"

"I didn't ask you Ola.. What was that you said?"

"The Agatus. They..they came to the farm. . . ."

A murmur rose from the crowd. Someone had just pushed a man to the ground. We were still in the middle of the road, in front of the chief's house, and the rest of the villagers were on the other side. The man that was kicked to the ground happened to be one of the hired laborers who had come to collect his pay from a member of our village who owned a huge cocoa farm. The Agatu man, with thick tribal marks on both sides of his face frowned in confusion as he struggled to get back on his feet. My uncle left our side, and ordered the whole commotion to a stop.

"Ah-hah..what is wrong with you all? Who pushed Nango?"

"Chief, those children already confirmed what we have suspected all along. Agatus are *ajeniyan*"

"Yes, look at them. They always carry those sharp *ada*"

"And, how come we don't see them in the market"

"Ah-hah, you are talking as if you don't know that they only feast on *eran eeyan*"

"Look at him, let him explain himself"

"Ahh, villagers, this man only came for his money o. Please fear God o. I don't believe this girl. Nango has been living with us for four years."

"Ehn-hen? So what? Who says you have to live for *odunmodun* with a people before you show your real color. Agatus are as bad as those *kobokobos*."

While the adults continued their unjust accusation at the Agatu man, the four of us stealthily picked our way through familiar footpaths of neighbors backyards to my aunt's house. The back door was left ajar, and before we went in, Olu pulled my ears, flashing me angry shots from teary eyes. She repeated the threat of a great punishment if I ever changed the version she told our revered uncle.

"If you ever tell him or Mama, I will ask that girl in your class to bring all her *abiku* friends to visit you. You hear?"

"And what do you think will happen to a girl who keeps lying and bullying young children . . . Ehn, Olu, answer me!"

Right behind the door was our great uncle. He held the wooden door wide open as each of us walked in. As I was passing through, head sunken to my chest, the old man lifted my chin with one strong finger, and said," Now Peju, tell me exactly what happened at the farm today"

GLOSSARY OF NIGERIAN WORDS/PHRASES

Abiku.   A spiritually errant child that is believed to have supernatural powers that make it possible to die and is reborn to the same mother

Ada.   Yoruba for 'machete'

Agatu.   Menial workers from neighboring Benin and Togo

Ajeniyan.   Yoruba word for 'cannibals'

Eran eeyan.   Yoruba for 'human flesh'

Iwin/oro.   Yoruba for monsters that roam the forests

Kobokobo.   Derogatory term describing the Ibos of Nigeria

Odunmodun.   (Yor) Literally year-in, year-out; a very long time

Tonmodesoko.   Confuse the child into believing it's still daytime; the teasing
     sunset

The Boy Who Did Not
Listen to His Mother

"Mama, we're ready!" Laolu and Yetunde rushed out of their room, their shoes laced, their faces scrubbed clean.

Mama tied the *oja* tighter on the baby who was already sleeping on Mama's back. She took one look at Laolu, her oldest child, put her finger in her mouth and wiped the corner of Laolu's mouth. "Must everyone know what you had for lunch? Didn't I tell you to wipe your mouth after every meal, hmn?"

Yetunde stepped on Laolu's sandaled foot. He squealed.

"Now listen children", their mother ignored the antics. "I'm going to the market to buy some things for the house. You, Laolu, take care of Yetunde and both of you make sure you do not cause any trouble while I'm away. Put your homework in your school bags and make sure you finish it in Jumoke's house. Are you listening?"

"Yes, Mama"

"Now, off you go to Anti Jumoke's house. Remember, no food. Especially you, Laolu, the bird that never fills up. You've just had lunch, so politely refuse any offer of food, or you'll be very very sorry!"

"The basket that never fills up...the pig that is always hungry.." Yetunde sang. Mama flashed her warning look. Yetunde stopped singing.

"Off you go." Mama ruffled Laolu's hair and patted Yetunde's cheeks as she sent them away, school bags slung over their shoulders, to Anti Jumoke's house six houses away.

Mama locked the front door and stood by the gate watching her two children platter towards their neighbor's house.

Laolu and Yetunde enjoyed walking around their street. There were too many things to see. There were old women just sitting in front of their homes, chewing kolanuts, shelling melon seeds or talking to themselves. There were old men calling out to one another inquiring about one thing or the other. There were children who, like Yetunde and Laolu, were on their way to friends' houses to do homework, to the market place, to the stream or any of the numerous after school chores that most children carried out.

Inside Anti Jumoke's house, Laolu and Yetunde sat by their accustomed places; Laolu on the little stool by the door, and Yetunde on the wooden chair near the kitchen.

"You children must be hungry." Anti Jumoke said, wiping her hands on her wrapper. "I must get you something to eat."

Yetunde was not hungry but Anti Jumoke's food smelt so enticing. She was tempted to say yes, but then she remembered her mother's warning that they were not to accept any food from anybody, not even Anti Jumoke.

"Thank you, Anti, but we've just had our lunch before coming here." Yetunde said, swallowing empty sniffs.

Laolu watched boys from his school play soccer with a Milo can. He wished he were with them. But he also remembered his father's warning that only lazybones play soccer after school when they should be doing their homework, or on the farm helping their fathers plant yam or even fell trees.

"How about you, Laolu?" Anti Jumoke's voice shifted Laolu's gaze from the activity behind the front door.

Yetunde shot her brother one of their mother's famous warning looks. Laolu looked the other way thinking Father does not want me to play football after school, and Mama dislikes children who accept food from other people's houses. But this food is too tempting. Maybe I shouldn't lose on both counts . . .

"Yes," Laolu said, avoiding Yetunde's disappointed face.

Anti Jumoke asked Yetunde once more if she really wanted to eat. And again, Yetunde refused politely.

Anti Jumoke left the children and went into her room to get ready for her friend's house. They had both agreed to go to the next town to attend a naming ceremony. Since she didn't know that Mama Laolu would send her two children to her house, there was no way she could have cancelled her arranged meeting with her friend.

Before she left, Anti Jumoke told the children that they were not to leave the house until their mother's arrival. She told ten year-old Laolu that he was in charge and should look after his eight year-old sister. She promised to be back before too long.

When Anti Jumoke left, Yetunde accused Laolu of being greedy.

"You are greedy! The greedy pig who is always grunting for food. The *miotiyo* bird!!"

Laolu licked the thick sauce off the drumstick. He crushed the chicken bone. Yetunde watched her brother and swallowed imaginary chicken marrow made real by the greedy sound in Laolu's mouth.

"*Miotiyo* bird!!" Yetunde hissed disgustedly. "You also have disobeyed Mama's order and I shall tell when she comes back."

Laolu threw the last of the chunky meat in his mouth before replying, "Yetunde, please, don't tell. I will do anything for you."

Yetunde shook her head vigorously, so strongly that the thread from her tied hair came off. "No, I shall tell Mama when she comes back."

"Tell. Tell, you hear and I will make Iyi beat you again like she did on Monday—Now, will you tell Mama?"

Yetunde started crying. Iyi was the bully in her class. All primary Three B pupils feared the tiny girl with a voice that was raspy as a masquerade's and commanding like the village catechist. The last time the bad girl had punished her was because she, Yetunde, answered a social studies question that the dull-brained bully could not. As a reward for answering correctly, the teacher had asked Yetunde to give each of her dumb classmates two strokes of the cane, and because Iyi was the original dull-head, four strokes.

Tired from weeping, Yetunde soon fell asleep, her smooth breathing regularly punctuated by deep sobs.

Laolu sprang from his stool, put away the empty bowl. He dumped the bowl and chicken bones in the big bowl few yards away. His school bag lay nearby but he did not settle down to do his homework. Rather, he made for the door to join his friends who seemed to be having a great deal of fun on the school field.

Then something happened to Laolu.

He suddenly felt very heavy in his limbs. It felt like somebody had replaced his feet with an elephant's. They felt like lead. His thighs felt as if they weighed tons of gold and he felt woozy in the head. He reached for the door, but instantly, he heard a loud noise like ten thousand bats flying in an empty cave and, swoo—ooo—shhhh-, Laolu felt himself flying through Anti Jumoke's window.

Outside, the boys were still playing football. They were shouting and screaming as the team played on, chasing the squashed Milo can around the dusty field.

Laolu's arms kept growing until it seemed they would be yanked from his shoulders. Huge feathers brown, black and white covered his lengthy arms and feet. Strong rush of warm air hit him in the face and he couldn't wipe the sting from his eyes now that he had no hands, just wings; great black, brown and white wings.

What in the name of his mother was happening?

Below him, Laolu saw tiny dots moving around a rectangular line like ants moving over a sugar cane stick. He recognized his friends playing football on the school field.

What was he to do?

His scalp itched, and immediately, great downs of black, brown and white covered his head and he couldn't scratch. He felt miserable.

Anti Jumoke's food rushed to Laolu's nose and mouth. He felt a burning sensation in his throat as his neck stretched and stretched and stretched.

A huge shadow darkened the sky and the boys instinctively stopped kicking the tin. They all looked up. They saw a creation that defied the creative impulse of the village's most imaginative story teller.

"What's that?" asked Ideolu whose foot still hurt from a Milo tin scratch.

The red, black, and grey bird was perched unsteadily on the most forbidden spot in the village—the century-old Iroko tree.

"What else, you fool; it's an *anjonnu* bird." explained Itayemi the renown *abiku,* who at twelve years was believed to have been born at least fourteen different times to the same mother.

The children scurried and disappeared into nearby homes, peeping only from the safety of closed doors.

"It's talking!"

"My name is Laolu, the disobedient boy." the bird said

More children had gathered by now. Women and men had long left their cane chairs and joined their frightened grandchildren. Once in a while, a boy would pelt the huge bird with stones, missing the target each time but drawing some attention from the crowd as the bird seemed to move its long thick black and white beak each time someone threw a stone at it.

"Please don't kill me. I am Laolu, the disobedient boy who has become a bird because he did not listen to his parents."

"Laolu?"

"Laolu, you fool! Yetunde's brother!!"

"No, it can't be; I saw him go into Anti Jumoke's house."

"Yes, with his sister."

"Will you children keep quiet and let elders think for a moment!"

All was quiet again, except for the mutterings from the parents.

By this time the sun, which only a moment ago was a huge bright yolk in the dazzling sky had turned an eerie glow the color of an overripe cocoa pod all over the village.

The village priest was summoned, and he stood in the safety of the church to behold the abominable sight.

The strange bird shifted again, uneasily, dodging a variety of missiles—milk cans, pebbles, catapults—pelted by curious children and some brave teenagers.

"Stop throwing things!" the chief bellowed. "That could indeed be Laolu! Call his father, someone!!!"

The giant bird that called itself Laolu moved its heavy build on the tree. A dry branch snapped. Several twigs fell to the ground. The bird latched its gnarled talons onto a thicker limb.

"I am Laolu, the disobedient boy. My name is Laolu, the boy who did not listen to his mother", it said again, hiding its long beak in its fluffy chest.

The sun had long gone, and Laolu was beginning to feel cold in spite of the layers of thick feathers that covered his body. Shivering, he whimpered, "I want my mother. Mother—-M-mmm-Mother, where are you? I am done for. Come get me, Mother, and I will never disobey you again."

Down, down, down below, several yards under the big Iroko tree, Laolu couldn't see anything but small dots of heads peeping out of windows. He shifted his weight to relieve his burning leg. More twigs fell off the Iroko tree.

More sighs escaped from the people below.

Then, from the dusky clouds, Laolu heard his mother's voice: "Laolu! Laolu!! Where are you? Where are you, my son?"

Up on the forbidden Iroko, Laolu heard his mother's call. He sluggishly pulled out his beak to make one frantic answer; then he suddenly lost balance.

And he fell.

Through the clouds, bright with light from countless glowworms.

Through warm clouds balmy with a hint of night rain.

He fell, sucking in mosquitoes, crickets, and drops of rain.

Finally, he fell into a swooping thud on the roof of his house.

The loud crashing noise split into a million stars near Yetunde's bed. She sat up on her bed. She looked around. She was in her room, and it was night. She saw Laolu asleep in his bed, his sleeping cover kicked, as usual, onto the floor.

Yetunde screamed.

Mama rushed into the room, her face swollen with sleep.

Baba ran in behind her, his face worried with a sense of alarm.

"What is it, Yetunde?" Mama knelt beside the frightened girl.

Yetunde looked at her worried parents, yawned and said, "Mama, I just had the most incredible dream."

The Torn Pages

The children were dressed for bed, and ready for their bedtime story. And, as usual, one of them would have to pick the story for tonight. Two days ago, the oldest boy, Didi, chose the story, and as usual, his brothers found the choice too boring. Yesterday's story was chosen by the middle brother, Sam, and as usual, they loved it. All three boys have a liking for ghost stories, and nothing beat the scary details of Mama's childhood stories. The youngest boy, Ife, has the responsibility of choosing today's story. His brothers begged him to choose one of their favorites.

"None of that about the goofy bear, Ife" one brother said.

"Please not another Ninja story. P-l-e-a-s-e" the oldest whined.

"Well, which will it be?" Mama asked Ife, who looked very confused as he sorted through a pile of story books.

"I don't know" the little boy cried

"How about I choose one for you, dear?"

"No, Mama, I think I know which one I want" the boy answered and gave a book to his mother.

"Oh – no"! hissed the oldest brother,

"Come on If, not the *Three Little Bears*, we're way too old for that"

"That's what I want"

"Please, Mama, make him pick another story. Or just tell us one of your childhood stories"

Their mother decided that the brothers would have to listen to the story picked by their younger brother, and that she would tell them one of her own stories the following night. She called on Ife to bring the book, and just as the five year-old was getting the book from the pile on the floor, the oldest, still furious at having to listen to the bear story for the upteenth time, snapped the book from his little brother, and, yes you guessed it, two pages were ripped.

"Oh-no!"

"Oops"

"See what you've done, you fool" the eight year-old yelled at the culprit who still had the torn pages in his hand.

"Thanks for ruining my story time, Stupid!" the eight year-old turned to Ife

"Don't blame me, blame the idiot"

"That's it, boys! I've warned you against name-calling. Sorry, but that's the end of story time" The boys looked perplexingly at each other.

" Everybody, to your room" their mother said, and got up to attend to the baby

The five year-old started crying. He slumped to the floor and still sobbing, put his thumb in his mouth. He soon got up, scooped up his blanket, and left for the room he shared with his three month-old brother.

The eight year-old kicked the nine year-old in the shin and ran to his room.

The nine year-old looked at the rumpled sheets in his hands, dumped them in the bathroom trash basket and went quietly to his room.

Soon, the whole house was quiet.

Somebody was knocking at his window.

Didi woke up and heard someone crying out his name. "Didi, open the door for us."

Didi quickly switched on the lamp by his bed. He squinted his eyes at the brightness of the light. He heard the voice again. And it was coming this time from the front door. He hid his face in the pillows and called out to his brother. "Sam, Sam, wake up! There's someone out there! Wake up!!"

He looked around his room. Sam was sleeping in the bed opposite his, with half his body hanging as usual, on the carpeted floor of their room. Soon, his younger brother would get up as usual, to use the bathroom, and he knew nothing would get him up before then. Still the voice beckoned from outside, "Open the door for us, Didi"

Didi remembered his friends in the boys scout, and how they were never afraid of anything; not even a spooky voice calling in the night. He pushed the pillow away from his face, swung his feet on the floor, put on his glasses, adjusted his pajamas, and tiptoed out of his room.

The voice droned on, pulling him toward the door.

Didi held his breath for a moment behind the front door. Then he opened the door.

Outside he saw two little boys, about five and three years-old, standing with their hands on the door knob. Behind them stood an old man cradling a baby girl in his hands. They did not come into the house. Didi held the door open wider, and motioned for them to enter his house. Still the strangers stayed outside. The younger of the boys looked up at Didi and said, "Please take us back home"

Didi looked confused. The old man still holding the baby on his shoulders, explained, "You see, we are lost. We were on our way home when suddenly something happened and we lost the direction."

"And then we found out that the two pages you tore yesterday held the direction to our house", the five year-old said.

"You must put us back on to those pages, or we'll be lost forever." The man and the two little boys chorused. The baby whimpered. Didi shivered.

"I-I'm-m-sorry" Didi cried. "I don't know where I've put the torn pages"

"You must try to remember where you left them before you went to bed," said the three year-old.

"And you must hurry and put us back before daylight", said the old man.

Didi scratched his head, squinted inside his glasses, and tried to recollect the event of the night before.

The strangers looked up at him expectantly. The baby whimpered.

"Very soon, very soon, baby, and we'll take you to your mother"

"See, my grandpa has to take my baby sister to the hospital. Our mother just died in an accident, and we may lose her too if you don't put us back. Please remember where you left the pages"

"I know it!" Didi jumped, his face spreading into a smile. "I know where the papers are!! Come into the house, and I'll rush to the bathroom. That's where they are" The strangers did not enter the house. Didi left them standing in front of his storm door, and ran into the bathroom.

In the bathroom, Sam was washing his hands in the wash hand basin. He frowned at Didi and silently watched as the older boy rummaged through the waste basket.

Didi threw out three lumpy soiled diapers.

He picked through wet tissue paper.

Finally, he pulled out the soggy remains of the torn pages.

"Oh-no!" he cried, slumping to the floor

"You know Didi, you're weird" Sam looked at his brother knocking his head on the toilet tank.

From the door, Didi heard the voice, this time, of the baby, saying "Open this door at once, you have no time left!"

Didi rushed out of the bathroom, scooped the wet sheets in his hands, and headed for the door. He tried to open the door, but this time the door would not open.

"You have no time left" the old man and the boys chorused, their voices floating through the room. Suddenly his hand was pulled through the little hole in the lock.

"Let me go. Let me go" Didi tried pulling himself back. The more he resisted, the more he was pulled through the knob.

"Let me go. I say let me go" Didi frantically thrashed about as he saw himself being pulled through the knob.

"Didi, get up! You have to get ready for school" Mama was standing by his bed, trying to pull up Didi from under the covers.

"Mama?"

"Don't you want to go to school? You have no time to waste. Come on, get up"

"Mama, you won't believe the dream I just had" *I'm not telling my den this one.*

"What? Were you fighting with some monsters?" Mama smiled, turning off the lamp by Didi's bed.

If you only knew Didi kissed his mother and left for the bathroom.

Whew! That was some dream.

The Motorcycle

My uncle was the headmaster of Leba District Central School, and the village people called him "HM". They all respected him a lot and I think it must have been because his house was the only other one, apart from the chief's, that was built with cement and corrugated iron sheets, unlike the mud houses with thatched roofs that littered the rest of the village. For one thing, he was the letter writer. The only person who didn't ask for my uncle's help in writing letters was the pastor, who probably knew more than how to read the bible and teach catechism. But my uncle was older and he must know more than the reverend. I also think those people reserved such high regard for my uncle because he was the only one, who made the illiterate villagers realize that other worlds existed beyond Leba. He told them of cities where people were of different colors and where rich men went about their business in motorcars that flew in the sky.

Life was really boring and uneventful, at least for me that I wished I were with those rich men flying in the sky. Let me give you a picture of a typical day in my uncle's household, and you would see my point of view. During the week, we started the day at half-past five with morning prayers at the village church. We then went about our morning chores, which for me was sweeping the front of the house. This was usually followed by a rush to the stream half-a-mile away to fetch water for our uncle's two wives. Each of us had to fetch three buckets of water and, if anyone were unlucky enough to drop his pot on our way back to the village, he made his way back to the stream alone. That of course meant that he had no breakfast since his siblings and cousin would have licked all the *ogi* and *akara* bowls clean. The unlucky person would quickly forget his hunger as he remembered that he had to be in school before the second bell rang, since that meant double the punishment meted out to other pupils; the price one paid for being the headmaster's child.

Our after-school hours were not relaxed either. Once we'd changed from our school uniforms into our tattered shirts and shorts, we would spend the rest of the day working in the farm about three miles from the village. By the time the moon appeared, our bones were usually too sore and weak to appreciate its crystal brightness. While Olu and other children listened to stories from their mothers, or simply ran wild playing hide-and-seek, we in our uncle's house had to rush to the corner table with the kerosene lamp wick pulled low and do our homework, sometimes frightened by our own ghostly shadows cast on the walls of the poorly-lit room. Later, with eyes stinging both from kerosene fume and exhaustion, we had to literally force our eyes open as we waited in a line for my uncle to inspect our homework. I always got everything right; but there were times I too have had to repeat a whole exercise just for missing one arithmetic sum.

So you can imagine our happiness the day Uncle Jonathan announced to his wives that he was going to Lagos. He said he was going to buy a motorcycle. That explained it! That must be the reason we had not been eating well for quite some time: our uncle had been saving all his money for this trip to Lagos.

Who wasn't happy that Uncle Jonathan was leaving the house for a whole day? Was it his two wives that the stingy man quarreled with everyday, or we his wards whom the three of them bad-mouthed all the time? We were all ecstatic to know that our common tormentor would be away for a while. Days before the actual journey, my uncle did something very strange: he gave his wives money to cook for the entire village! A whole goat was slaughtered and we ate more food than we'd ever eaten since we'd been living with Uncle Jonathan.

Everyone attended the party. The pastor, the school teachers, Sikira the village gossip, and even Omoawo, the herbalist whom my uncle had forbidden us to have any contact with because he was the Devil's own servant. Everyone of them wanted something from Lagos, from shoes and safety pins, to cigarettes and shirts. In the end, my uncle agreed to buy a gramophone record for the chief, and a sewing machine for the pastor's wife.

The Chief and four other elders prayed for the success of "HM"'s journey. I didn't understand all the fuss about my uncle's trip to Lagos until I was told that he was going to be the first person from Leba to go that big city.

Uncle Jonathan thanked the Leba people for their good wishes saying that he needed the prayers to ward off the evil forecast in letters received from some friends of his in Lagos who had warned him about the dangers abounding in the city. The village pastor assured him that the city couldn't be as bad as his friends had portrayed. My uncle told the pastor that he was not afraid of any lousy Lagos rascal, and that he was going to prepare very well for those good-for-nothing beings; after all, have they not just prayed for him? And didn't his God defeat all those stubborn pagans of the Old Testament? So what would a Lagos vagabond do to an 'omo Olo'un'. Anyway, my uncle the "HM" seemed resolved to teach those Lagos rogues some lesson.

How did I know? The day following the send-off party, my uncle sent me to his tailor to collect the *agbada* that he had had sewn for the Lagos trip. It was a voluminous tent-like creation with two huge pockets hidden inside. These arm-length pockets were designed specially for the fourteen pounds that the motorcycle was going to cost, and the ten pounds that he had collected from the village chief and the pastor.

That was not the only preparation. Uncle Jonathan shunned the barber's shop in our village, going instead to the more prestigious one at Arigbajo, fourteen miles away. He wanted a hairstyle he had seen in *The Morning Post*. The finished job parted his hair in the middle, as if a caterpillar had just raked through a thick forest. He covered it up with a specially made cap. We knew he was embarrassed by the style because it made my uncle resemble some of the hooligans at the motor park.

The day arrived at last and we all escorted Uncle Jonathan to the railway station. You should have seen the man! He was so happy, smiling at everyone and actually greeting people!!

Uncle Jonathan was to be gone for at least twelve hours, so my brothers, my sister and my cousin all decided to have a good time the hours my uncle was away. Even his wives went out to visit friends in the next village. We on our part went to the nearest farm instead of the back-breaking one four miles away.

We didn't do much at the farm either. We just visited all the citrus trees and shook out as many tangerines, oranges and grapefruits as the number of marks Uncle Jonathan had inflicted on us with his cane. We sucked out ripe cocoa pulps and spat out the seeds, then climbed kolanut trees, plucked several pods and made footballs with the largest of them. We soon got tired of kicking fruits and returned home to play real football at the soccer field. We played for a long time, and neither side scored any goal. Hunger and tiredness dampened our enthusiasm, and we agreed to do a penalty score.

Segun was the goalkeeper and he dived for the ball as it tore its way into the goal post. No sooner had he caught it than he dropped the ball, spat out sand, and raced from the field, crashing into the pastor who was headed toward our house.

Other children rushed past me.

Curious, I stopped to check.

Then I saw him.

Uncle Jonathan wore a look that resembled the pastor's face whenever he was listing the sins of Leba people; however, unlike the pastor's ironed cassock, my uncle's *agbada* was the ghost of what the tailor had sewn . Worm-like veins pulsed furiously in two gnarled hands that held together a torn portion of the robe . My feet refused to obey the messages flashed by my scared brain and I waited on jelly limbs for the blow that I knew must resound on my face.

Uncle Jonathan walked past me grunting and muttering.

I couldn't believe he didn't hit me! I rose from my knees and wobbled my way home.

Segun stepped on Kunle's feet and in annoyance, my brother shoved his thin elbows in our cousin's side. In the commotion that followed, I eased myself into Segun's vantage position. He pinched my sweaty back with his dry nails but I didn't budge. I had to find out what had happened to Uncle Jonathan's motorcycle.

"All the time I was sure I had the money with me because I could still feel the bulge against my body," Uncle Jonathan was saying to the pastor. "The money was there, I knew it was there, under my *agbada*"

"They said they have so many vehicles that one can spend a whole year counting them!" Lagbaja, the chief's messenger enthused, and the pastor silenced him by reminding the man that only a lazy fellow would spend precious time doing a crazy thing like that.

I could imagine my uncle getting so impatient with those two. He interrupted the pastor as the reverend was saying something we could not understand. In a tired voice my uncle told of how he finally got to the depot and was about to cross the wide road when a man in a fine uniform kept waving at him from the middle of the traffic.

"Do you know the man?" the pastor asked my uncle.

"I thought at first I knew him and was going to talk to him in our dialect when all of a sudden, the man frowned at me, shouted an abuse and waved in another direction."

Uncle Jonathan started laughing all of a sudden. There was silence as his cracked voice rang out loudly cracking to a cough . He stopped abruptly.

"HM, what is the matter?" we heard the pastor ask.

I couldn't hear my uncle's response because Kunle was nudging me to create some space for him. Segun snapped his fingers at the two of us. That meant he would skin us alive and, frankly, I didn't mind. Something had happened to our stingy uncle and I must hear it all.

"A traffic warden, that's what the poor man was. He was directing traffic, carrying on his duty, and Mr. Jonathan Titilola, honorable bushman from Leba, thought the policeman was waving at him!" Uncle Jonathan's voice hissed through the keyhole.

"So I entered the showroom, saw different brands of motorcycles and chatted for a while with the salesman as to the one I liked best. The man allowed me to test two of the vehicles, and, in the end, I made up my mind for the Triumph"

"Ah HM, I thought you were going to buy the Vespa?" the pastor's voice was beginning to sound like on the pulpit.

"Ehn, but where is the Fespa?" Lagbaja asked.

I pressed my chin against Kunle's head, hedged Segun's chest away from my neck with a sharp butt of my elbow, and strained my eye to have a better view of the scene in Uncle Jonathan's bedroom. All I could see was the blurred outline of the tobacco tin on my uncle's windowsill.

"So they gave me their voucher to sign. I finished signing and put my hand in my agbada to pay the money.."

You could hear every suspended breath in the room and behind the door.

"And I reached for the money and my hand came out of a large hole that those Lagos bastards have cut in my *agbada*. And then I looked at the back of my right hand and heard myself say 'Jonathan, is this not your hand you are looking at . . . ?'"

GLOSSARY OF NIGERIAN WORDS/PHRASES

Agbada.   Voluminous robe commonly worn by men in most parts of Nigeria

ogi and *akara.*   Common breakfast food in most parts of Nigeria. Ogi is made from shelled, soaked and ground cornmeal; while akara is fried black-eyed bean fritters

I Saw Her Coming Out
Of a Dark Hall

I've been looking for the file that has the beginning of a story I was preparing on my mother. I'd written up to seven pages, and now I've lost it. I really can't tell when or where the disk got lost, so I'd better start all over. How I got the news of her death. How I looked back on the days I spent with her. How I now regret not spending enough time with either her or my father. I remember I used to wonder what my mother really looked like. How much did I really know her not having lived with her in my formative years. Now that was more than forty years ago.

That also was when I became conscious of my mother; you know. That knowledge which comes from a depth so unfathomable as to be eternal. I remember the first time I saw my mother. It was at night. She was dressed in her favorite 'up-and down'. I must have peed in my underpants because there she was, pulling out the wet pants and fixing me with dry ones. All along I pretended to be sleeping. I guess even at that age, a tad over three years, I was a little ashamed of wetting myself. I drifted back to sleep.

The next time I remember seeing my mother, and recognizing her as mine was when she and my father would come into our room. They would come in the doorway, and just stand there looking at us. And I knew she was my mother. We were never introduced formally, but I knew if ten thousand women were lined up, I would pick her up in a heartbeat. There was something that reminded me of her. You know the feeling that you've met this person even though in your conscious life you've never. The same with my mother. Each time she left my room to wash the ammonia laden beddings, she was always humming my song. Or rather, her song for me. "Labisi o Labisi

> Labisi omo jeje
> Labisi o Labisi
> Labisi o eh
> Labisi o o seun. . . ."

And so on. I never knew how the song ended until years later when I would sing it to myself each time I missed her. But that's another story. . . .

It was the same song that she told me she sang to me when she was carrying me inside her. She was not a stranger to pregnancy, and being her seventh baby, she was so sure she would carry even this one to an effortless finish. At that time there were two older sisters in boarding schools, two other ones in elementary schools, my two immediate older sisters, at five and two respectively made her a very busy housewife. So she had no time for a difficult pregnancy. Not during the seventh time. During her prenatal trip to the hospital, the Irish midwives informed her that she was carrying a breach baby. She was however reassured once the sisters 'turned' the baby. On her way back to the quarters she shared with her husband, the baby 'turned back' to its more comfortable gut ripping, back-breaking position. My mother told me she didn't tell my father at home what the delivery staff told her. About her baby being a breach, or as the Yorubas would call it, an 'Ige'

Why not, Maami , I asked pulling the third gray strand off her carefully plaited hair. That was my after dinner chore. And at that time forty years ago, it must have meant something for her sense of wellbeing to not carry a head full of white hair. After all, her mother went to her grave at almost one hundred with less than twenty gray strands.

"Why Maami," I asked again, pulling at a slightly grayish strand. I soon lost it.

"Because, your father's people don't like children born that way."

She turned this way and that, searching for more gray hairs. All the time I was looking at her reflection in the mirror on the table opposite her bed. I soon found a slightly gray strand lurking behind shiny hair. I pulled, and the hair came off with no struggle. She rubbed the spot where the culprit strand once occupied. Her hand reached out to receive the jar of Petroleum jelly. Through the mirror, I watched my mother apply a thin film on the spot.

"But they told us in school that such children are very lucky in life"

"Your teachers must be right because you would have been killed in my people's place."

I took the jar back from her, and placed it back on the table carefully setting the can next to the stack of family pictures, a worn out Bible and different containers of worm expeller, malaria fever and other medication that cured the assortment of illnesses a family with children was subject to.

I didn't need to ask her why her people wanted to kill me because she had told me several times before. She came from a group that didn't welcome babies who came into the world in other position different from the one they ordained was the most natural. That meant any baby who walked, kicked or sampled life with any body part other than the head, was evil. In the days of her mother, such babies were destroyed; so I knew what she meant when she called me lucky. At the end of every hair-plucking session, I was always rewarded with my theme music, or what in those days I called my personal anthem.

Labisi o, Labisi

That was the song I yearned for when I discovered blood in my panties at the boarding school, away from my mother. I started my period away from her. Three months later, on holiday from school, she noticed that my school list featured a new item: sanitary pad. She hugged me, and I was embarrassed to fully return the hug. That meant she knew I could be pregnant, and the thought was not a comfortable one, since my cousin was home with us pregnant at sixteen, expelled from her school, and renounced by her father, my mother's half brother. She took me to Kingsway and bought me three packs of sanitary pads. I didn't ask for much information, as my older sisters had filled me up on everything I needed to know on menstruation, and most especially, what happened when people 'missed' their period. She asked me if it hurt, and I told her yes, like hell. She chuckled. I asked what was funny, and she calmly informed me that what I called pain was nothing compared to what women suffered when they had babies. That did it for me. I made up my mind I would not have children if it hurt more than my menstrual pain. All she did was hand me my new menstrual pads, gave me a gentle tug on my shoulders, and smiled. "You will have children, and you will tell me it was painful. But, Labisi, you will have babies. You'll see. Labisi o Labisi . . ."

I wanted to tell her what I knew already about girls and menstruation. How the girls in my dormitory at school would stink up the aluminum and cement bathroom with their bloody rags. Before I saw blood on my bed sheet, I used to wonder how people could wash rotting blood with their bare hands. Those girls did. And the rest of us who must use the wash hall at the same time had to inhale the putrefying steam in the crowded bathroom. I wanted to tell my mother how I hated those girls, who incidentally also happened to be from the countryside. They would chat unabashedly in the bathroom, wash the rag with same *Premier* soap they had washed their body with. I knew when my own time came, I would never use cut rag, would definitely not wash anything in front of total strangers, and I was going to use sanitary pads, like all the girls from affluent homes were using, even if I was not that well off. I wanted to tell my mother about all this, but I knew she would try to remind me of how in the days of her mother, women cut rags during their menses. I also knew that she would have looked at it from a humorous viewpoint. She would retell the story of the woman from her place who was banished from the village and instantly divorced by her husband because she had used her menstrual rag to cook a sumptuous meal for the unsuspecting besotted man. My mother had told me that the woman soaked her menstrual rag and used the solution to cook pepper soup for her man. That the woman had followed the instruction of a witchdoctor who had assured the harried woman that her husband would never send her packing on account of her barrenness. I thought of the story, and decided against telling my mother abut girls and their toilet habits Telling her all of that would probably reveal things I would not consciously let on, like girls doing things to themselves under their netted beds, or asking other girls to share their beds. That would be as embarrassing as discovering blood in my underpants.

She didn't harass me about boyfriends, even after enrolling at a private school for my A-Level and with no special friend in tow. What bothered my mother about me was what she called my temper. She and my father always included my bad temper as top priority on their prayer list. She would tell me of what happened when people, especially girls, lost their temper. "They end up alone, Labisi. You don't want that to happen to you."

What did happen was that I breezed through school with little difficulty. Graduate school went easily too. I didn't have to miss my mother because I went to school in the same town in which she and my father lived. I saw them every week, and all through special holidays. Sometimes I saw her twice or more a week, especially whenever my ulcer was acting up, and the time I had my knee drained at the university clinic. During my ulcer attacks, which she immediately explained as an offspring of my anger, she came to my room in the graduate hall with home-made *akamu* from barley and millet. A week's menu of nothing but millet gruel and milk gave me a long respite from the painful gastric discomforts. She felt guilty at my distended knee because she believed I inherited her arthritis and the resultant weak knee. I didn't feel too bad about that since her presence was the ultimate balm I always needed.

Sometimes, the political upheavals of the seventies on Nigerian campuses necessitated a rather erratic academic schedule. Needless to say, students were sent home following series of demonstrations, rallies, and much damage to public and private property. The university sometime remained closed for more than a week during which I enjoyed my mother's ultimate care and presence. When it came time for me to go back to campus, a mere five miles from home, she would accompany me all the way from the potholed street of our neighborhood, through the dusty ride to campus. Her presence was a healing balm. This balm eased so much pain during the years following NYSC (National Youth Service Corps), ultimately leading up to marriage, again, away from her. Thank God she made the long journey to attend the wedding. Knowing the psychological implication of marriage without the full blessing of a mother must have propelled my mother into marking her presence at the wedding of her seventh child, the very child that stubbornly kicked her thin legs into the world years ago, in an Ibadan hospital one stormy night, instead of rolling in, like all normal babies.

What didn't happen to me was for my mother to be present at my own baby's delivery. She was not there because she could not be there. I was nearer in thought than reality. Physical distance was our common enemy. Add to that a struggling newly-married couple making ends meet in an incredibly small cubicle of an apartment, somewhere in cold, rural Illinois. Talking to her on the phone two hours after a most painful ordeal, I told my mother that indeed what I just went through defied any comparison. I told her in a very weak voice that birth pain was truly the grandmother of known physical discomfort. She didn't say 'I told you so'; rather, she began worrying about my postnatal care:

"Who is going to cook for you?"

"Do you have people who know what to do with a new mother?"

"Do those people have things to clean the baby?"

"Who would press the baby's cord?"

"Oh Labisi, my Labisi, ah . . . how I wish I were there. By the way, what did they do to the afterbirth?"

"Maami, what do you mean?"

"I mean, who buried it for you?"

"Oh, that; I don't know"

"What are you telling me, Labisi? They were supposed to have given it to you for proper burial." Her voice sounded so desperate. I couldn't tell her that the delivery staff had asked what they should do with the placenta. I remember looking over splayed legs at the doctor's capped head, his eyes dancing like loose discs between my legs. A nurse was holding a blue nylon bag under the delivery table, and I felt the mass slid out of me into the bag. More fluid drained noisily into the pan under the table

"So what do you want to do with this?" The doctor had asked, tying the end of the bag with a thread.

"Nothing." I had answered, assuring them that they could do with that body part whatever they wanted. The nurse had hesitated, hoping I would change my mind. When I still insisted I didn't want to carry home a rope of flesh, the doctor explained that some of his maternity patients were particular about the afterbirth. A number of them had taken the piece home with them in a special container. I told him the hospital could use my placenta for any research or dump it wherever they wished.

"'Bisi are you still there? Hello-o"

"Oh, Maami, yes I am here. I was saying that everything went well with the delivery. Aside from the pain"

"But where is the second birth? What will you do with it? Do you have someone who can help with the burial?"

"No, Maami"

"But you have it?"

"No. I mean, they put it in a bag"

"Go and get it from them."

"Maami, the ground is frozen. It's snowing, so I can't bury anything. It's not that easy here Maami."

"You can dispose of it . . . No you shouldn't. It's an abomination. Oh, ehn, I should be with you now. . . . Don't those people bury their second birth?"

"No, Maami. They throw them away."

"Oritse mobuwo! They do what? Don't do that. It's not good. What do people from home do? Aren't there others from Nigeria that live around you? Go to them, they'll know what to do"

"Maami, there are just the two of us in the whole town."

"Hello?"

"Hhhhhhsh -"

The line was mercifully disconnected. But I knew even then that she would still ask what became of the baby's afterbirth.

I was angry when we got disconnected. And I was also mad at her for bringing up the afterbirth topic. I had wanted to tell her how hungry I was after the birth, and how, after I buzzed the nurse's station, the kind lady at the desk nicely reminded me that the kitchen was closed, but that she would see what she could rig up for me. She was true to her word because in ten minutes, she brought in my first meal after a thirty-six hour labor: a can of cola, and a cold turkey sandwich. I remember gobbling down the food, ice and all. I also remembered chuckling to myself in anticipation of my mother's mortification upon learning that her seventh child, her most fragile offspring gave birth thousands of miles away from the nurturing care of her family, and salt upon injury, was given something COLD to swallow. She would have prescribed pepper-soup made with fresh 'obokun' or catfish. Or, knowing that I had a weakness for dried fish would have suggested tilapia seasoned with all the native spices and herbs. She would have reminded me that every new mother needed to cleanse her system with those ingredients. Not cold soda. Definitely not bread and cold roasted turkey. She would have cried if she'd been told. That was what I forgot to tell her during all that debate on the aftermath of the afterbirth.

Maami never asked me what became of the afterbirth the next time we spoke on the phone. I knew she must have had a long discussion with my sisters, and they would have explained to her that in America, people do things differently; including ways of disposing an afterbirth. I'm sure she didn't believe much of what she was told, but because she was concerned about my health and general well-being, she carefully avoided any talk about placentas.

Three births later, she still didn't ask what became of the second birth. And I never encouraged such line of discussion. I'd rather listen all hour-long to her enquiries about life in America. Her surprise at the time difference. The fact that they had just come back from church while we were getting breakfast ready. That her grandsons were still sleeping while she and their grandfather were busy at one thing or the other in the village.

"And what will you do when you come back from church?"

"What meal will you prepare?"

"What are you doing tomorrow?"

"Did you say it's snowing there? *Oritse,* it's hot like hell here! And NEPA just took the light."

Each time I heard her voice I always ponder on Edward Said's discussion of the dilemma of the émigré. He describes the situation as a separation of the soul from its source. I felt the same way each time I talked to my mother. There were too many things to say, in such a limited time that one tended to merely rush over topics. There I was trying to maintain a continuous discussion with her, and on the other end, several thousands miles away, a retinue of relatives wanting to say a quick hello. And in the midst of the confusion, the line was disconnected. And usually, until much recently, that was a line I kept a vigil to connect. I've never wanted to keep away from home for this long. Actually, I've never intended to live outside my home country having lived much of my growing up years away from my natural habitation—my mother.

Taken together, I lived with Maami for just six years after which I grew up with her sister in-law for a total of five years. Five formative years during which I learnt about house chores and accompanied my aunt to the farm on Friday evenings, and to the market on Saturdays. During those years, I saw *abikus,* and noticed the differences between boys and girls in my class, and in the choir, and I also became aware of the difference among Moslems who lived in Ifo station, the pagans who inhabited Old Ifo and the Christians made up of the few families perched on the hills of Okenla. It was in those years that I learned to fear the dark, especially as described by our imaginative primary two teacher. It didn't help that my aunt's house was a few yards away from the churchyard. That was also a time when the only light came from an assortment of kerosene and palm oil sources. In those five years in the small Anglican primary school, I attended Empire Day celebrations and Girls Guild meetings. I feared Akintola. In the five years, I came across *Lambs Tales from Shakespeare*, and *Aworerin*. I saw Awolowo writing in the sky. Those years introduced me to the Church of England catechism, and familiarized me with the slogan, *Go-On-With-One-Nigeria*. I feared and hated Ojukwu. I learnt to distinguish *abikus* from normal children. In those years, along with other children at school, I learnt and yearned desperately to have the one chance to hide in the ditch once the siren went off.

After those six years, I went off to the boarding school, where I spent another seven years away from my mother. Seven years during which I grew from spindly legs and all head to spindly legs and all head with a size thirty-four chest.

Of the twelve years away from her, those first five were the most unforgettable. It had all started with a weekend trip to my father's ancestral home. Like most city workers, my father, a warden at a Lagos hospital would travel the two-hour drive to their village on an average of twice a month. Usually he traveled with his cousin, a pathologist who had his own clinic in Surulere. The cousin's mother was my father's aunt, and at the time of this story, is still the oldest living relation, having celebrated her seventieth way back in 1965. However, on one such visit, the two cousins decided to introduce their children to the village. Now with the children from my father's side, we were vaguely familiar with poor people, having seen some of them in the hospital environs, or at motor parks, or simply in front of the bus stops on our way from the church in Agege. My cousins on the other hand were what Nigerians called 'Ajebota'. Their mother being a European also meant her children, as half-castes were looked upon more favorably than regular Nigerian kids. While we lived in the residential section reserved for junior and mid-cadre workers, my cousins lived in a better part of Lagos, with their own cook, gardener, and their Opel Kadett car watched faithfully by their uniformed 'mai-guard'. There were three of them; two boys, and the only girl, the apple of her father's eyes, Oluronke and I were friends. It didn't matter that she attended an exclusively private school in Victoria Island, and took lessons at a ballet class, the two of us had so much in common. She didn't speak Yoruba, and even though I understood a little English, and could not carry on a lengthy conversation in that language, we spoke and exchanged lengthy information, and needless to say, were happy to be included on the entourage to the village along with my two older sisters.

We had arrived at the small hilltop settlement sometime in the evening of a Friday. We were scheduled to leave on Sunday after church. It was our first time at the village, and we were so thrilled to find so much space to romp and frolic. We invaded the plantain orchard while the grown-ups updated each other about events over freshly tapped wine brought in by farm helps mostly hired from neighboring Cotonou. We didn't care about palm-wine or food for that matter; we were simply taken in by the sheer expanse of space. And we rolled on mud floors, watched each other use the backhouse, visited other family elders and chased chickens, lizards and guinea hens all over the dusty paths.

Saturday went as fast as the day before, and soon, it was time to go. And that was the beginning of my long sojourn away from my mother. By Sunday afternoon, my *ajebota* cousins were ready to go back to their comfortable residence in Lagos; so when their father called out, they rushed out excitedly, their hair now shaggy and their limbs itchy with bites from multitudes of mosquitoes, gnats, and *kotounkans*, the tiny bugs you could hardly see. We too had bumps on our dark skins, but they didn't show as glaringly as on Oluronke's light skin. My father followed suit and called out to his children, myself and two other older sisters. My sisters had not had their fill of the village, so they told my father that they wanted to stay on at Ifo. Thinking they were joking, my father called again. And again his daughters reiterated their first excuse. Life was no fun without my sisters, so predictably, I too stayed back. My father went alone with his cousins and we spent another fun-filled moonlit night at my aunt's place.

My mother arrived very early the next day, She reminded us that it would soon be school time, and we needed to come back home to Ikeja. Her three daughters looked their mother in the eye, and said no. She told them that if she left without them, she would only welcome them back on holidays. Her three daughters jumped happily and laughing agreed that they were ready to live in the village and would see their mother on holidays. They left to play in the newly discovered playground of 'Agbo ogede'.

Being a woman of few words, my mother left, came back the next day with all our school materials; khaki uniforms, Quink, Kandahars, pencils, and erasers. Like she promised us, we saw her again, only during holidays. Of course I wanted to go back home once the orchard routine became a bore, but you could not win with my mother's sister in-law, my impressive and impossible aunt. I did everything to get me back to my mother, a mere thirty-three mile distance, but nothing came between the agreement sealed on that first day. I once ground a yellow chalk and put some in my eyes so my aunt could think that I was jaundiced with yellow fever. She laughed at my attempt, and I got a pull of the ears for daring to blinden myself. Apparently, the specks from the chalk just clogged my lashes like a badly applied eyelash.

Soon my younger sister came to join us in the village, and frankly, that made life a lot happier. Even our youngest sibling, my parents' only son could not bear the absence of his favorite sisters, and he too joined the ever increasing brood in Ifo. However, their sojourn did not last long since my mother could not bear living without any of her children. At that time, three daughters were in different boarding schools, and there were five of us living with my strict aunt. The two younger siblings soon left after staying at the village for only two years. My two sisters lived in the village for two and three years. I lived the longest, staying there for five years. I got in in primary two, and left after successfully completing the first school leaving examination. That took five years.

My mother didn't come with me when I left for secondary education in a boarding school some seventy miles away. My father came with me on that first day. I remember in the bus taking us to Ile-Ife that my father talked about how I was going to be the best I could ever be. That I could become a doctor, a lawyer, an engineer; anything I set my mind on, I could become. I knew I was going to be a doctor long before I left Okenla because I had seen the picture of my father's cousin in the papers where it said she was on her way to England for 'postdoc' I remember that Sunday afternoon in the village after church, my father's uncle, the proud great uncle of the niece going to London was radiant with happiness as the whole extended family celebrated the success of yet another daughter of the soil. Then in primary five, I knew I was going to make my father proud of me. It was as if I wanted to make up for his not going to college. So I told him in the *bolekaja* speeding the one-way lane to my school in Ile-Ife through the forest environs of Ikire, Gbongan ,and Ipetumodu. My father handed me over to the principal of the historic school, and he promised to take a very good care of me. I don't remember crying after my father left; but I know that if it had been my mother that came with me, things might have been different. For one thing, she would have insisted on following me to the dormitory instead of leaving me at the principal's house. Knowing my mother, she would have helped me make my bed and set up things with the matron.

But she didn't come with me to Ile-Ife that day because her only brother, Uncle Temisan, was in detention somewhere in an Ikeja cell. I knew about that two months later, during the Easter break when I went home. Because of the Ojukwu palaver, anyone who looked like an Ibo was subject to any assortment of punishment. Although she was not a Yoruba, my mother was well-known on our street in Ikeja , but when the civil war broke out, and my uncle sought refuge at his sister's house, our neighbors became paranoid, and told the vigilante that roamed the streets that there was a Biafran man in the neighborhood. That freaked my mother out. She had to prove that the so-called Ibo man was her blood brother. That they should disregard his violent temper; it had nothing to do with being a 'kobokobo'. My father had to intervene before his brother-in-law could be released. He had to prove that he was the one that invited my uncle to come down to Lagos when the Midwest was getting too dangerous.

I haven't told you yet, but my uncle in his childhood days was called "Yellow", on account of his very fair skin, something not unrelated to too much blood mixing in their ancestry. My uncle's nose was rather straight, not flat like most men from his group. My mother on the other hand, was your typical Itsekiri woman; dark-skinned, average height, slender build that defies metabolism as it ages, and a graceful head tapering a long neck She was the oldest of three, and he was the youngest. According to my mother, their mother spoiled my uncle to the point that he didn't do well in school; really did not have to do anything as he was from a famous family whose history dated back to the glorious days of Nana.

Before he came to our house in Ikeja, my uncle Temisan was employed as a civil servant and he lived in the same house his parents had raised him and his two sisters in the dusty market area of Okere. When he arrived at our house, after losing his job in Warri , Uncle Temisan still didn't feel at home. An unassuming man, he couldn't understand why his first wife left him, and didn't feel any compulsion for another wife. However, when he realized that he would have to be his own man in this Yoruba place, he agreed to marry a woman from the Delta hinterland. They fought all the time. It was hard to say what always triggered their argument, but it always ended the same way. My uncle's wife garrulous and rude attitude, seemed too uncouth for my sensitive angry uncle. That was the situation when I left for school with my father.

Each time I'd left home, I always promised myself not to be too far away from my parents. I remember when I came back home from Ile-Ife, after my secondary school education, I prayed not to be accepted at a school too distant from Ibadan where my parents lived. Fortunately, Iwo, where my A-Level school was situated was a shorter distance to our house than my Ife school was. But in spite of the closeness, I still didn't get to see them as often as I would have liked; the rigorous schedule of the boarding school made it impossible to go home unless for emergencies. However, since I was blessed with a very healthy system, I didn't get sent home before the scheduled breaks.

I just had a dream the other day. It reminded me of another dream I had few days before my mother died. In the first dream, I was looking for my mother, and she also was searching for me. Don't ask me how I knew she was, because I just knew it. However, there I was standing in this very dark hallway looking for my mother. It was as if I were in a grove in the thickest part of the forest. The strangest thing was that the grove was also a hallway and right in front of me my mother rushed out of a cave, saw me, said something that translates into "How dare you keep away from me for so long?" and struck me in the chest, right where my heart was. Rubbing the sting on my chest, I started crying and explained that it was not my fault; that I didn't mean to stay away from her for sixteen years. She looked me in the eye, pulled me to her breast, and while I silently cried she comforted me saying "I know, Olabisi, I know . . ." I woke up knowing that bad news was on its way to me through some bad hallway.

I didn't tell anyone about the dream. But two weeks later I had the other, more ominous dream. In this one, I was standing in front of a room. Like a hotel room. Inside was my mother standing by a bed, and unpacking; as if she had just checked into the room. I was surprised to see her there and I asked what she was doing in that strange place. Strange because standing next to her was my younger sister, who had died ten years earlier. She asked me to come and live with them. Still standing in front of the room, I asked her again what she was doing in the same room with my sister; didn't she know that the girl had been dead for ten years? My sister, who in life was full of life and harmless mischief, winked at me with a look that said 'I've got her". My mother smiled and calmly told me that I would soon come and join them. I knew there was a dead person in that room, and that knowledge alone gave speed to my jellied feet. I ran from the room, feeling the warmth of my mother gnawing at my back.

I told my husband the dream, and we decided to call home. That was on a Monday. I went to school, taught my classes, came back home eight hours later, took the boys to their various after-school activities, came back home and cooked dinner. At the end of the day, typical of any other day for me as a Nigerian working mother living in the United States of America, I was dead tired. When I woke up from my before-sleep nap, it was three AM, already past breakfast time in Nigeria. At any rate, the nice gentleman who had one of the three working phones in my father's village would have left for Ifo Station to begin his daily rounds of sickly homes needing his pastoral care. In a strange way, I was secretly glad that I couldn't get home. Not because I didn't want to talk to my parents or my aunt; far from it. My gladness stemmed from the fact that one hardly received any good news from home, and each time I called and the line kept ringing busy — which by the way did not mean someone was on the other end using the phone — I quickly replaced the phone, satisfied, albeit momentarily, that I have fulfilled some haunting duty. Another reason I was relieved that I wouldn't be talking to my parents that day was because one week before I had the dream, we had received a call from one of our friends at home informing us of the death of my husband's younger brother. So you would agree with me that I've had my cup overfilled.

Or so I thought.

I didn't feel too elated on my way to school on Wednesday morning. Usually I would tune to my favorite oldies station in Cincinnati where *Kool and the Gang, KC and the Sunshine Band* among other groups returned me to Idia Hall, the UI Theatre, Awba Dam, the parties and all the favorite haunts on the campus of the University of Ibadan. Those songs always brought memories of stolen moments, brief disappointments, students riots and the classic chants of "Ali mun go!" in front of Trenchard Hall. But that morning on my way to school, the radio was doing "Requiem" by Mozart. I love classical music, but it is not the first thing I want to listen to on my way to teaching a bunch of African-American college students. Something upbeat prepares me better mentally, like my UI music. On the other hand, when I'm going to church, chamber music, the Gregorian chant or any choral from Medieval England seems so appropriate. But "Requiem"? I changed the station, and for the first time since I've been tuning to the Cincinnati station, it kept jamming into other unwanted stations. I tuned off in frustration.

Eight hours later, driving the twenty-one mile distance home, I tried the station again. Twenty-five minutes later, I was still stubbornly tuning trying to stabilize the station when I pulled into my driveway. A car was parked in front of the house, and I recognized it to be the rector's new automobile. It didn't strike me as anything strange seeing the reverend lady in my house; after all she was noted for her thoughtful surprise visits to her parishioners' homes. I didn't bother taking in my bags and all the paraphernalia that accompanied me to school. I went in and saw my husband sitting down in his favorite armchair. Then I didn't notice his hands. If I had I would have guessed that something was amiss. You see, Paul would lock his hands in a tight fold such that the two resting on his lap—always his lap—resemble a plastic heart with gnarled veins on the back of the hands masquerading as the heart's arteries. He folds his hands that way whenever he is tense about something, or someone has just delivered some terrible news. I came in greeted the reverend, and sat down wondering what she had come to do. I actually believed she had come to see how we were doing.

I asked about her mother. Oh she's fine, she replied. The youngest boy threw a toy at his older brother, an eight year-old, who was trying to steal it from him. The toy landed on the reverend's shoulder, and full of apologies, I rose to retrieve the plastic ninja. Another thing bounced on the piano. The good lady said something about boys would be boys. I was becoming really irritable and flashed the culprit, the eight year-old with a look that promised to roast him and his brothers later on. He picked up the football, dragged his four year-old brother behind him, and disappeared into their room. The reverend lifted her eyebrows in wonder at the sudden calm. Paul was still sitting on the armchair. And his hands were still locked in a heart-grid. I asked if she wanted anything to drink. Oh, that's alright, Bisi. Don't worry. I went back to my chair by the piano. I never suspected any bad news. Then she said something about some bad news. Bisil'mafraid I'vegotsomebadnews. Just like that. The sentence just dropped out of her mouth. Then I relaxed, thinking it must have been one of the church members, especially since one was rushed to the hospital few days before for an emergency open heart surgery. And the good lady knew that my husband and I were in the prayer group that kept each other informed of prayer requests of parishioners and non-members alike. What a pity, we've lost another one. My mind was still commiserating with the family when the reverend's next sentence jolted me back to my living room.

"Bisi, I'm afraid I've got some bad news. I'm sorry but your mother has passed on"

I cracked my knuckles and wondered where my mother was passing through. Where was she going? Passed on. To where?

I felt the lady standing behind me, her hands on my shoulders in readiness for a showdown she was so sure was imminent. I just kept imagining my mother passing. And right there I hated all euphemisms that wouldn't deal the blow when you needed it. Passed on. Passed on. Perhaps the good lady meant my mother, whom I delayed speaking to on the phone two days previously, whom I saw in two bad dreams, the woman whom I was just going to talk to on the phone tonight,

"Yes, Bisi, Mama died. She died two days ago." The phantom on the chair had left his seat, and was standing beside the reverend.

"Bisi , Mama is dead"

That's what I like about the guy. He's always hated euphemisms too. He hates when people refer to him as 'visually impaired' and has consistently re-minded them that he was not visually impaired; that he was as blind as a bat. He feels that if the sufferer can handle their fate, there is no moral excuse for an on-looker to not be honest in their description.

"I'm so sorry, Bisi. You see Paul was afraid to be the one to tell you, so he called your friend in Illinois who contacted me and advised that I be the one to tell you"

"Yes, Darling I had to call *Egbon* Peter because I honestly wouldn't have known how to tell you that Mama is dead."

Wow, my mother has died. In Ibadan we used to substitute funny expres-sions for that simple phrase. I remember occasions when I've had to tell other students, or listen as other people were told:

Your mama don die
Ya' mama don mud
Oh, sorry, na your papa; in don quench
I hear say somebody don disappear
O ti fi'le bora bi aso
O ti deni ana
O ti . . .
"Bisi..?"
Ibadan images melted and I saw Paul's mouth still moving.
"Bisi, Mama is gone . . . I'm sorry."

"Yes Bisi . . . so so..sorry."

Thank God, Paul made the distinction cleaorer, and allowed the blunted roughness of the reverend's couched phrase to churn my heart's wall, sawing the shreds with a sharper edge.

Days following the news, I floated through my crowded life carrying on as if my mother was still alive and at home with her beloved husband of over fifty years.

I couldn't cry for days. School numbed me to the extent that I was able to carry out regular duties efficiently. Soon people began to look at me rather strangely. And they came up with tons of advice:

"Don't lock it all in."

"You've got to grieve for your mother."

"Bisi try to cry."

"You need to cry."

"It's good for your sanity."

"Don't be brave."

And so on . . .

I wanted to tell all the well-wishers that I was okay. That there was nothing to relieve the frozen ache that had sought refuge on top of my brows. Or the heaviness that perched on my shoulders . . . Nobody could understand that I needed some superhuman intervention to tease away the lump that forever rolled across my chest, just above where my mother had struck me. I sent 'Thank you' cards to countless greetings and gifts, especially from the Nigerian community who perfunctorily enclosed checks and sometimes, raw cash in their envelopes mindful of the ritual back home where the bereaved are always thought to need money. So, I listened to their advice, welcomed their condolence visits, and carried on with my life as an over-chored mother of four young sons, wife of their equally frazzled father, and teacher at two different colleges in a small town in Midwest America. Still the ache persisted, the pressure on my chest intensified, and I finally took one of the host of advice and arranged for a memorial service. Paul came up with that advice, and together we planned a beautiful service with the good rector.

I cried a little during the service, and once uncontrollably in the faculty lounge of my school. I hated that display because of all the places I wanted to splash my sorrow, that school was the last on my list. That was when I decided to write about it. To see how what was hurriedly swallowed could be regurgitated in order to relieve the endless discomfort. And I think that was how I began the story in that disk that is now lost. I started by explaining that I'd been made to swallow some bitterness that defied the childhood quinine my mother used to faithfully dispense to all her children once a month to combat yellow fever. Only this time the fever just wouldn't go, because I had not been bitten by anopheles mosquitoes. Bad news, unlike yellow fever, defies any prophylactic prevention and this brand of bad news just rips through the gallbladder, punctures the bile duct, and presto, you have an endless gush of the bitter fluid.

That was what I typed and saved on that diskette. Now it's lost. I'll probably find it one of these days; but then I might not need it again since I've captured all the record stored on that disk. Well, almost all.

GLOSSARY OF NIGERIAN WORDS/PHRASE

Kotounkan.   Small gnats with very itchy bites

Ajebota.   Children from wealthy homes where butter is a frequent dinner feature.

Kobokobo.   Ethnically derogatory term used by Yorubas of Nigeria for the Ibos.

Maiguard.   Hausa colloquial for the night watch man

Agbo ogede.   Banana plantation

Egbon.   Respectful term used by the Yorubas to address someone older, and more experienced

Oritse.   Itsekiri word for "God"

Oritse mobuwo.   Itsekiri for "God, I beg you . . ."

Your mama don mud.   Pidgin for "Your mother is dead"

Ya mama don mud.   Nigerian pidgin for "Your mother is dead"

O ti fi'le bora bi aso.   "He/she has been wrapped up in soil." Yoruba euphemism for "he/she is dead"

O ti d'eni ana.   Yoruba for "he/she has become yesterday's person"; euphemism for " he/she is dead"

Signatures

The checks came today, and as usual, Ayo checked the signatures. Somehow, her signatures don't always look alike. How come, she wondered. The 'A' on the check she used to pay her daughter's boarding fees is a picture copy of the signature on her college graduation certificate. But here, look at the one for the mortgage; drastically different, as if she had signed with her left hand. Why isn't her signature as steady and constant like Dipo's? His are so illegible like they've been for the past thirty-four years she has known him.

She used to tease him about his interesting scrawl, which he fondly called a labor of love. He would start by elaborately tilting the tip of the pen awkwardly to the right, then a few moments of non-writing with the pen still rigidly poised over the document. In a flash, the tip of the pen dashes across as if the hand that holds it suddenly loses control. It jerks to a stop, and with a final dot, Dipo's signature is done, picture perfect in all its ugliness.

Ayo always believed her husband's signature would be easily deciphered by any Chinese graphologist. It resembles a thin snake with a decapitated head stretched to an unnatural straightness by some unseen force hiding under the reptile's thrashing tail. Thirty-four years, and Dipo's signature has remained the same. No change, no thickness to the lines, no blotching on paper, no bleeding pens, her husband always signed documents with the same personalized Parker pen.

When they first met thirty-four years ago, Ayo could still remember being fascinated by the young manager's ceremonial signature. She had just been offered a job at the ministry of labor, and for the first time she had to sign a car loan form. To her surprise, Ayo found herself scribbling across the form the same way she did it on those scholarship forms years ago at the boarding school. So will this be her eternal hand mark? It's acceptable to sign like that at the boarding school; after all she was a highly imaginative girl, what with a very enthusiastic art teacher who encouraged all possible artistic expressions. And she remembered playing with each of her five names, and always undecided about what was going to be her final signature. Eventually, the time came for the O-Level exams, and on her form she had combined the first syllables of her five names, and the last syllable of her surname. So, while her friends, all boys, easily dispensed with the task of filling forms, she spent a long time agonizing night worrying about her signature.

Ayo now recalls that what really bothered her forty-something years ago was not that her signature extended into the margin of the form, but that she probably ought to have retained all of her surname instead of using the last syllable which by the way was a 'Fa'. Maybe she ought to have signed Orukotan instead of 'Rukotan. Well, she signed her name like that for ten years after that O-Level episode until her encounter with the bank manager who made such fuss over her uninteresting signature.

Ayo checked the checks again. She couldn't move much as both arms were being fed God knows what, and if she moved to her more comfortable side, the drip may spill. Still, she could see the checks where the good nurse had left them, spread on a reading table hoisted above her knees on the bed. The scrawls sometimes take on souls of their own, like the one on the check for her youngest son's boarding school. Right now, the character above her printed name looked like ET's eyes with a kite's tail. Whatever they were giving her for the pains must be responsible because, granted her signatures were always irregular, they were never comical and certainly not like ET's eyes. She always signed with a neat scrawl across the document. Her father used to describe her signature as cursive written by a drunken hand.

That was what he said when he saw her marriage certificate thirty-two years ago. Ayo believed her father never really forgave her for deleting his family name from the characters on her signature list. Well, what else could she do? Dipo had never really drilled her into learning a new signature. She simply believed that once a girl was married all things must become new. Old things — including ways of doing — consequently had to go. And go did her premarital signatures. She unconsciously assumed one of her numerous signatures. Actually there are as many as six or more of the variations. Good thing about Dipo's name is that his last name is shorter than her maiden name.

She was still registered as Dipo's wife, even though it's been two years since their divorce. At first, she was confused about what to call herself. At home in Nigeria, she probably would have reverted to her maiden name, but she has learned a lot since she's been in this country. Her colleagues at the research office all still answer their ex-husbands' names and thought nothing about it. What really plagued her was how to sign her checks and other documents. It became rather uneasy especially when she had to sign their joint checks. She solved that problem the second month after the divorce by opening an account in her own name. Even then she had used her father's last name as hers.

And that was wrong. To think that it took a breast cancer encounter for her to realize that her life had drifted from one person's existence to yet another. Never hers. *Thinking about it all, reminds me of an assignment one of my college professors gave us several years ago, way before the advent of gynocriticism and women's studies. The man had asked the class to write nonstop for ten minutes on who we really were. At first none of the eighteen students did anything. We just looked at the Saul Bellow look-alike, and wondered what happened to him and his wife that morning. Anyhow, being professor Mater, you had to write, and write we did. I remember that cold November morning in Iowa. I remember among other things that I summarized myself as being an extension of my Nigerian community to the extent that kinship became important inference. So, I was my father's daughter, my community's daughter. So, what am I now? My ex-husband's divorced wife? My three grown up children's mother? A reliable researcher and funny individual . . . Or my poor plain cancer riddled self . . . ?*

There is a knock on her door. Ayo's eyes slowly open. The light in the room is too bright and she blinks. Her daughter comes on. She is the oldest, and at thirty is already a successful attorney. She has insisted that she be given the power of attorney for her mother. Ayo remembered when she came out of the intensive unit and was being wheeled back to the recovery room, that the surgeon was saying something about transferring all mental responsibility to someone very capable and trustworthy. Or that if she didn't have one the human resources section of the hospital would hire one for her. That was almost six days, and she still had not informed the hospital about who would have the power of attorney.

Banke tiptoes to her mother's bedside.

"You look fine mother."

Ayo knows Banke is trying to sound brave; just like her father. Dipo would never show any sign of pain-physical or emotional. It must be a genetic thing. Banke didn't even let her know when she started her period. Maybe her father knew. To think that she Ayo was so busy in the graduate school and didn't even notice when the girlish Banke crossed the threshold. No talk of sanitary pads or tampons. Not even pregnancy and Condoms. All Banke wanted to tell her mother when Ayo came home from graduate school was how she passed one Bee and represented her school in another regional competition.

Then she turned eighteen, and it was too late to speak to her of boys and sex, and contraceptives. Way too late because Banke already knew of the evils lurking in boys and sex, and pills. She was worried but didn't tell Dipo because they had begun to go their separate ways. With the two boys, there was little or no problem. Their father took them under his wings. Since he was an accountant, he decreed when the boys were only six and nine that Ope was going to be an architect, and Dele would be the family's physician. Like his ugly but constant signature, Dipo's boys lived up to their father's aspiration. Now just twenty-two, Ope is an intern with a building farm in Atlanta, and Dele is one of the youngest residents at a hospital in D.C.

"Mother, how are you?"

Ayo raised her lids. Banke is still standing there. Tall. Very dark and striking, just like her father. As usual, dressed as if heading for the court room.

"Still tired, what do you expect?"

"Has the doctor talked to you yet?"

"What about?"

"He was saying something about em . . ."

". . . Power of attorney?"

"Yes."

"So?"

"Well—Have you decided to whom the power should be transferred?"

"Yes. Me."

Banke meanders her way through the confusion of wires, tubes and syringe plastics on the floor. She removes one of the many vases of flowers on the only chair, places on them on the window sill, and sits down.

"Mother, you must realize that—"

Just then the doctor walked in. Alone. Ayo's neck stiffened involuntarily. When that happened, something is not right. What was odd was the doctor coming into her room alone.

"This must be the daughter you have been talking about?"

"Yes."

"Hello."

"Hi."

"What's up doctor?"

"You know what Ayo. Have you chosen someone?"

"Power of attorney? Yes. Me."

"Be serious. This is the nineties. We need someone who will take charge of all legal ramifications and complications."

"Yes. And that person is me."

"Look, Ayo, I am hoping for a miracle cure. Your cancer has metastated, yet the new approach is so daring that we will need to be discharged of all obligations. We want your approval which must be conveyed by a legally appointed officer. It's the law."

"You are just wasting your time Dr. Knells. I am still in possession of my mental abilities. The cancer has not ravaged the brain yet. So bring me the form and let me sign it."

"Mother, please let me assume the power of attorney."

"No, you are my daughter. You can go to the next room and tell the patient that you wish to act as her attorney. To me, you are Banke the girl who started her period silently without telling her mother."

Banke quietly followed the doctor outside.

See? I have defeated her yet again. Sometimes that girl acts too Caucasian for my liking. At her age, no boyfriend; Oh spirits of my ancestors, I hope she is not one of those women who . . . no, that's unthinkable. I never even saw any special friend with her. . . . Oh my poor daughter. It is Dipo's fault for insisting that we send our only daughter to the prep school in England. The poor child was sent there from Nigeria when she was only nine years-old. At that time we were all in Nigeria. Then came the job offer by the World Bank, and we all left for New York, with the exception of Banke who later came to join us from England. Even at thirty, she sounds like a character from one of Jane Austen's novels. Accent too crisp. Attitude very British, and whenever she took her to her office in D.C. her colleagues always wondered what such two different women had in common. Ancestry, you fools! Better still, heredity.

The door closed quietly, and Ayo glanced at the form left on her table by the doctor. She pressed the knob on her bed and cranked herself to a comfortable position. Her arm felt drained of whatever they were pepping her with. To think a very unnoticeable act like pressing a knob could surge off energy draining down her torso and evaporating into the thick blankets before escaping into the room through her toes. She needed another surge of power to sign the form waiting defiantly on her table.

The doctor came in this time with a nurse who wheeled in a tray of prescriptions for Room 222.

"Where is Banke?"

"Ban-Kee? You've upset her. She is waiting outside."

"Tell her to come in."

"She is very upset."

"Upset my foot!.. She will get over it. I don't know why she has to behave like a white, ah! Just some home truths and she's—That's funny."

"What is?"

"Banke. She never shows emotion. You know she's the one with her head tightly screwed up. In Nigeria, that may be an omen that I won't leave this hospital alive. Maybe she sees something I can't see."

"Ayo, you know what I see. I see a very tired lady. So take your tablets, lie back and rest. We'll sign the papers tomorrow."

"No, no Doctor. Who are you kidding? I am signing this form now if it takes my last breath."

The nurse assembled the different medications on Ayo's table, looked over drips and changed tubes, and then she left the room.

Banke walked in sniffing.

"Banke, I am sorry but I need you to witness so please—"

Banke moved nearer the bed. The doctor removed one of the tubes on each of Ayo's arms.

"Are you sure about this?"

"As sure as the cancer waltzing through my bones."

Doctor Knells brought a pen from his gown. Ayo shook her head and instructed Banke to open the drawer by her bed. Inside was a black and gold tipped pen with Ayo's initials.

"That's the retirement gift from my office. See? It bears my initials."

The doctor replaced his pen and put Ayo's classic felt in her numb fingers.

"How will any one believe it's your signature, Mother?"

"Oh well, they only need to assemble my past signatures. One of them should resemble this. By the way, did you get in touch with your dad?"

"Yes—I mean no, he wasn't at his home. I left a message on his answering machine."

"How stupid of me. Your father must still be enjoying his endless honeymoon with your friend. Can you hold the form please?"

Doctor Knells held the right corner of the form, and Banke held the other. The two of them waited for four full minutes while Ayo stubbornly read the rights in a weak voice. And then she scratched the top margin of the form with a pen. When she was convinced that her gold tipped pen was ready to be used, Ayo signed the form.

Without a father, without her recently divorced ex-husband, without the knowledge of her two grown up sons, with her sniffling grown up daughter, and with all her cancerated cells, and lacerated bones, Ayo welcomed her true signature. Nothing about the present one shows Dipo's influence, no trace of her father's roots, no lazy scrawls signed by a tired and harried mother, no hurriedly signed signature as scrawled in the midst of a PTA meeting. This time, she is signing her name and giving her own permission to these strangers to do with her cancer whatever they want. Just with her cancer mind you, not with her.

Doctor Knells looked over Ayo's shoulder, gently placed the form on the dinner bench on top of Ayo's bed. In a gentle voice he turned to his patient and said,

"Ayo, we need a last name. This is incomplete. We need a full signature, like the one on your admission card."

"Well Dr. Knells. That was my ex-husband's name, and don't think I am going coocoo or whatever you Americans call it—No—Banke let me talk. I know what I am doing. Leave my name as is. No last name."

"You can't achieve anything with an incomplete info."

"You are the one wishing for a miracle. I already know that my cancer is a goner. My husband is somewhere in the Caribbean with my daughter's friend, and my sons are yet to know of my illness. My only daughter has yet to find a husband, so how is an incomplete name going to change all that?"

The doctor rushed to his patient's side, held her weak hands in his strong ones, looked her in the eyes and said.

"It's okay Ayo. We'll go ahead with the operation, with your signature — as is."

"Okay."

Ayo slowly eased her hands out of the doctor's grip. The physician touched Banke's shoulder and quietly left the room closing the door gently behind him. A nurse came in and replaced the oxygen tube in Ayo's nostrils. Banke kissed her mother's cheeks and left the room shortly after the nurse.

The Punishment

When my aunt called me that afternoon, I knew I was in trouble. I had just come back from school, my cheeks still burning from the sting of Teacher Ade's slap.

"Titi –"

"Yes, Mama –"

"I said come here –"

"Yes Ma –"

She was standing in front of me, blocking the doorway leading to the room I shared with three sisters and our cousin.

"Come here –"

She lifted my face with her hand and let out a sigh as she traced her forefinger gingerly over the raised welts. I dropped my schoolbag and dropped my chin farther down my chest. My aunt raised my face, and with her hands lightly around my shoulders asked me what had happened to my face. I started to explain by telling her precisely how it happened.

"What do you mean Teacher Ade said you did not close your eyes. Did you shut your eyes? –"

"No –"

"So, Teacher Ade did not lie when he said you opened your eyes? Answer me! –"

"No –"

My aunt started muttering to herself and went inside her room, across the hall from ours. I was still standing with my schoolbag by my feet when my aunt emerged from her room. She had removed her head-tie and transformed it into a sash around her waist, and her face had changed from an irritated mother to that of an angry woman. I knew what was going to happen. Those of us who lived with her recognized that demeanor.

The last time my aunt's *gele* doubled as an *oja* was when she beat up Tongo, the tallest man in the village. The unfortunate man, one of several Togolese farmhands, owed more than a month in unpaid cigarette fees when he asked for two sticks of cigarettes. My aunt refused to get him any more 'siga' until he paid at least half of the money. The man reminded my aunt that he left four wives at home, and would not tolerate a single woman bothering him about ordinary cigarettes. Mr. Tongo didn't take the hint when my aunt whipped off her head-tie, swirled it into a quick sash around her waist.

" –You should be happy that I even come to your place to buy anything at all. In my country, women like you . . . -"

The next thing we heard was Mr. Tongo, all six feet of him crashing through the rusty aluminum wall of our kitchen. He didn't see my aunt's hand head for his face; however, because my aunt was much shorter, the blow landed on the man's chest catching him unawares, and catapulting him to the dirt floor. The man tried to regain his posture but his legs wiggled and he crumbled into the earthen oven, sending ashes floating over everything. I recall that my aunt kept hissing all through the episode, and we children giggled our way out of the man's thrashing limbs. He looked so pitiful wobbling in that mud oven.

"I said follow me-!"

My aunt's angry voice jolted me out of my reverie. We went through the back-door, past the kitchen and through the bushy path in front of the outhouse. Along the way we saw Mama Bunmi, our neighbor whose house faced the school fence. She was drying her laundry when she saw us, but having been my aunt's neighbor for over twenty years, she just looked on and said nothing. My aunt dragged me along the dusty road that led to the schoolroom.

Teacher Ade was still in the room when we burst through the door of Class 2B. He was putting books in his old portfolio in readiness for home. Before he could say 'hello', my aunt hopped on one of the wooden desks, knocking off the inkwell in the process. I cowered by the doorway, watching on shaky legs.

From my doorway view, I saw Teacher Ade's hand reach out to protect his left cheek. He could not. My aunt's second slap sounded like when Mama Bunmi was beating the pile of *aso-ofi* that her clients brought to her for cleaning. My aunt leapt to the floor and delivered the third slap on her way down. All the time the short man kept shouting and rubbing his cheeks.

"Ah Mama Titi—What ah—This is unheard of—What—Oh, my face— Me? Ah—My life—Ah, Mama Titi—please-"

My aunt rushed to where I was standing mesmerized. She shook me up, and pushed me into a chair in front of the humiliated man who was also trying hard to subdue his anger. His bag lay on its side, under the table where my aunt's surprise attack had flung it, spilling sheets of paper, colored chalk, pencils, one Parker , and a Kandahar ink bottle.

"What could she have done to deserve these marks on her face? -"

"But, Mama Titi, she was disobedient—she did not close her eyes when we were saying the dismissal-"

"Oh. And how did you know that? By closing yours? If you had shut your own eyes like a good teacher should, would you have seen her? -"

"Still, Mama Titi, she disobeyed-"

"Disobeyed? She disobeyed and you needed to make her obey by crushing her face bone? You did wrong. This is not punishment; in this village, it is called highhandedness. We know you don't have children, but you should know that when a bulky, ill-spirited, stocky man like you slap a broomstick like my little girl, you are bound to inflict a heavy injury—"

And so on.

Teacher Ade was still stuffing his school belongings in his bag when we left Room 2B. On the way home, my aunt acknowledged greetings from other women who had gathered in front of the schoolhouse.

"What happened, Mama Titi?"

"Titi, what's wrong with your face?"

"Ah, some people have no fear of God in them-"

"Is it that *oloriburuku* teacher-"

My aunt sent me home ahead of her, intent to give a detailed account of all that transpired inside Room 2B.

On my way, I drifted back to events earlier that day, during lunch when Teacher Ade demonstrated one of his daily wicked routines. One sickly child, whose parents were known to be very poor, had come to school, again, in tattered uniform. His khaki shorts were torn at the seat, his white shirt faded dirty yellow from frequent washing with caustic soda soap. Teacher Ade always reminded us at the close of every school day, to wear clean uniform, wash our mouth and remove 'jiggers' from our feet before stepping into his classroom. Ganiyu came in that day, while we were already doing the catechism class, and since our catechism took place in the church. Teacher Ade could not do anything to Ganiyu ; however, after the class , and once inside our classroom, he called the boy out and ordered him to be given twelve strokes of the horse whip. All this because Ganiyu whom he called 'keferi' disgraced him in front of the Reverend—and in a house of God. The boy quietly took his punishment and the last three strokes rent his already ragged shorts. The class watched as blood ran out of Ganiyu's exposed buttocks.

The day before that, the same teacher had asked me to give two strokes of the bamboo cane each to all nineteen pupils who could not respond instantly to his arithmetic quiz. By the time I finished, my arm ached, and my neck hurt and I wished I had answered wrongly and been caned myself, instead of getting the mental test right, only to have to suffer raising my arms nineteen times two times, and turning my neck this way and that way. The most frightening thing was facing my enraged classmates at the end of school. I was busy planning my escape route and did not notice that I had not closed my eyes while the short evil man was saying the Grace.

The very short pupils usually stayed in the front row. Being the tiniest and shortest primary two pupil, I was on the outer edge directly opposite the teacher. When my eyes made four with Teacher Ade's, I could not blink or wink, I just kept a frozen glare, my hands still folded in a prayerful clasp.

"School dismiss-"

"Hurray!"

"Titi, to my office!"

Everybody knew what that meant. Those that had it in store for me after school for carrying out Teacher's request earlier that day during Arithmetic went home happy in the knowledge that my punishment had been fixed.

"Goodnight, Teacher-"

"Goodnight. Greet your parents-"

"Goodnight Teacher-"

"Ganiyu, change that rag, or stay at home-"

And so while my mates hurried on home, I went with much trepidation to see our teacher. He didn't ask me any question, he just reached out one thick forearm. And I saw stars.

The stars multiplied, the ones in the center brighter than the others.

I saw more stars.

Then my face exploded as hot tears rolled down sore cheeks.

I was still trying to hide the weals when I saw my aunt by the doorway. I greeted her and thought I could rush past her. I didn't know that I had tilted my head toward my chest. That was when she called me.

The Fever

I've heard them say it is so different in the city. They said you have cars the size of our school field. That children catch the bus to school. That people swim in blue water, right in front of their houses. Some people buy their fish, vegetables, cigarettes, firewood and kerosene from a big two-story building, not an open marketplace like ours. That inside the building, you climb some metal steps to go from where they sell foodstuff to a table that has almost any kind of children toys. Hhhmnn! They even said that city children don't know what a farm looks like because they all live in *petes*, and the only space is left for flowers and plants trimming the edges of their houses. The most fascinating story I've heard about the city is the hospital. They said people sleep in the hospital. That children have their own rooms with tables full of some of those toys from the big in-door store. That when children are taken there, kind people give them toys and sweet. And that's why I wanted so badly to go to a hospital. It would be a change from the hard existence at my uncle's house. I also don't like the idea of all primary school children going to the market-place next week to go and line up the street for a big *oselu* from the city. You must have heard that the premier is coming to our town. No, let me put it right: the man is going to pass through our district, and all of us pupils in area schools would be waving the green–white–green flags in the hot dusty roads. I went once; to welcome some white bishop of our district church; and oh, did we suffer! I sweated so profusely that after a long while, my sweat tasted bitter. That's how long they roasted us children on the roads. So, when Teacher Oluwi told our class that we should get our fine uniforms ready to meet the premier on his way from Lagos, I prayed something would prevent me from going. And my answer came yesterday.

We have a dispensary here in the village, but the hospital in the city, I've heard them say, is very big, very comfortable, and with no mosquitoes. Imagine that! Not even a single blood sucking mosquito. You should see my entire body; mosquito bites have decorated the back of my neck, my whole back, arms, and thighs. Don't talk of my legs and feet; ahhh, they look like the spots on a crocodile's back. My uncle told me the bites make one strong. He said that while he was growing up in his father's house, the mosquito bit every exposed part of his body, and that it was the itch from the bite that took his mind from any challenge the following day might bring. I found that confusing, very much so. I don't like talking about my uncle. He confuses me. Not just his eyes that bulge out of his forehead and pop at me from behind a pair of thick eye glasses; or his nose that flares so widely you could see worm-like veins dancing around wet nostrils. His large tongue sucking imaginary objects out of evenly spaced teeth always forces my mesmerized gaze from his face to the snake stretching his throat as his Adam's apple moved this way and that way. My uncle confuses me to no end, and I always dread having to be called to his presence.

As my luck would have it, I developed a very bad fever yesterday. No, let me put that better: I realized I might get sick with fever yesterday when I came home from school. Why is it a good thing to have fever? I'll tell you why: it is the possibility that I might not be going for the rowdy Empire Day celebration at the dusty marketplace. I always end up with headaches, body ache and just sheer weariness from walking the two mile distance between our school field and the marketplace. But , perhaps the greater reason I look forward to sickness is because I live with my uncle, a man I don't like talking about, so scared he will hear me from anywhere. In my uncle's house, we all work like donkeys, that is, with the exception of Keji. I will tell you about her later. Anyway, we work like *ketekete,* but must not show any sign of weakness whatsoever. However, being the village dispensary man, my uncle has stipulated that once anybody's temperature goes beyond 100 Fahrenheit degrees, then it is time to stop working. I know that what I have since yesterday is over 100, and that is very, very dangerous. I know this because I am in primary three, and our teacher already told us about millipede and centipede, the very week we learnt about Fahrenheit and Celsius. And I remembered that day in class 3A that one of our classmates had a very high Fahrenheit, and Teacher Oluwi sent him home immediately. He told the rest of us that Ajayi was carrying a very bad parasite inside him; and that was making his blood boil, resulting in a very hot temperature. So, I know when a Fahrenheit is not to go beyond the normal, which according to Teacher Oluwi is 98.7 degrees. The way I've been feeling since yesterday is not in the periphery of 98. Whenever that happens, Teacher Oluwi said you must have fever.

So, I came home, because Teacher Oluwi sent me home shortly after lunch break, and told me not to come back to school until "Your stingy uncle take you to a proper hospital." His very words. I dare not repeat it to my uncle, because that would start a long ugly fight between two men who can't stand each other.

Actually, you can't blame anybody for not liking my uncle. I already told you that I am rather uneasy about him. But Teacher Oluwi's feud with my uncle is common knowledge in the village. You see, my uncle's second wife is Teacher Oluwi's younger sister. The same woman who abandoned her husband and ran to the village to marry my uncle. I still don't know how it works with grown-ups. See, in my uncle's house, there are three wives. The first woman, whom everyone knows as the oldest wife, is also my own aunt. She took charge of me at the death of her only sister, my own mother. She hasn't yet told me anything about my father; that is not to say I haven't heard enough earfuls from my uncle about "the pig" "the ingrate" "the irresponsible *keferi*"; all names describing my real father. My aunt, whom I call Mama, out of respect, not because she is somebody's real mother, is an easy going person. She sells food at the primary school, and in spite of my uncle's sometimes rude remarks about her, is the one that gives me money for things we are asked to buy in school. She has been married to my uncle for a long time, I think fifteen years now, and she has no child for him. He calls her all kinds of names, but she ignores him and goes about her business of feeding him and the rest of the family. The very year my aunt brought me to her home, was the time her husband decided to marry another woman.

Teacher Oluwi's sister had just been married off to a man she did not like, but whom the family felt was good enough for her by virtue of him being a headmaster. She herself was not an illiterate, being the proud owner of a First Primary School Leaving Certificate. From what I heard said around the village, she ran away from the headmaster's house one morning, and the next day, my uncle arrived home from a visit with a strange woman as his wife. He had warned Mama that he could no longer tolerate a barren woman. He called her "Broken Pot" He said he needed a water pot that could still hold much water. I said it once, my uncle confuses me. Anyhow, he told Mama she could either leave or accept Teacher Oluwi's sister as her co-wife. Mama ignored him and left for her stall in the market where she sells farm produce on weekends. Seven months after she arrived at my uncle's house, Teacher Oluwi's sister gave birth to a baby girl, whom my ecstatic uncle named Keji. Rumors flew around, I heard, about the legitimacy of the baby. Some mouths in the village suggested Keji was not my uncle's real child; that her mother must have been pregnant for another man before marrying my uncle. Teacher Oluwi publicly called my uncle impotent. My uncle knocked out the man's teeth; but not before Teacher Oluwi explained to stunned villagers that the war robbed my uncle of his manhood.. I forgot to tell you that my uncle fought Hitler during the Second World War. And they said that he was shot in the groin, and that must have explained why he could not make any baby with any woman. Mama probably knew all about it, but kept quiet because she didn't want to embarrass him. He dotes over Keji in ways unexplainable; especially for a man who does not know how to console children when they are sad, or when they are so tired from working so hard. Keji's mother has no child aside from her, and that is why the rumor about my uncle not being able to father any child seems so likely. I just wonder why a beautiful woman like Keji's mother would want to spend eternity with my uncle. I can understand my aunt whose main concern is to see me succeed in life. For that reason, she is ready to suffer to any length, and probably, she can do that better as a married woman, I don't know. All the four food vendors at our school have husbands; there is not a single one of them that is unmarried. Maybe that is why my aunt stays married to my uncle; I don't know. All I know is how grateful I am to her for making life in my uncle's house a bit bearable.

I started by telling you all I've heard about the city,. and how I want to go there myself, not having been there before. At least not that I can remember. My aunt told me that I was born in a real hospital, not like the dispensary we have in the village.

"Your mother was a very successful trader. She had you in the city hospital. Then you decided to come out walking, when every normal child drops on their head."

"Then what happened, Mama"

"They came and called me. The nurses, they called me from where I was standing, outside the place where you were born"

"And then?"

"And then, I . . . don't make me talk, Child, I took you from the doctors and brought you here."

Sometimes, I wished she had taken me elsewhere, anywhere but this village where there is one of everything: one small church with corrugated iron sheets for roof; one small school with mud walls and peeling paint situated on a long patch of lush green land; one small river two miles away, one tiny burying ground with faded grave stones and newly dug graves awaiting headstones. There are seventeen households in our village, mostly mud and thatched roofed, each with its own backyard of assorted outhouses, vegetable patches, washing areas separated by rusting aluminum sheets and rotting wood pieces. My uncle's house is the only one with iron sheets for a roof, like the newly decorated church. He came to the village after the war, and refused to continue to work for the colonial government. He used to say that what he saw in Burma made up his mind about any long-term association with the white man.

"Oh, if you see what these *kongba* eyes saw in Burma"

"Oh what did you see, pray tell us"

"To think that we are after all the same"

"You and who, Mr?"

"These *erankos,* the white man. *Sege.* To think that we both worked for the same man. *O mase o*"

"You and who?"

"For which man?"

"If only you knew what I know . . . but what's the use, you won't understand."

Like I said, the man confuses me. He would start talking about Burma and Calcullta, then, he would stop. Just like that. In the midst of a sentence. So people started calling him *"Aromental".* Teacher Oluwi said that is what happens to someone who steals other people's property. I don't know what he meant. Unless he is referring to Keji's mother. You know I told you she used to belong to the headmaster. I don't know.

Yesterday, I noticed that my temperature had gone above the normal Fahrenheit. Was I happy. The night before I went to school, my uncle had sent me along with Taiwo—the other boy living with us—to the farm that was about three miles from the village. Keji had been banned from doing any farm work. My uncle told Teacher Oluwi's sister never to send Keji anywhere outside the village because she was his life. The only proof of his manhood. He said Keji was his reason for being alive. Well, Taiwo came to live with us one day after one of my uncle's extended relatives brought him to the dispensary. He had almost cut off his ankle by accidentally stepping on a trap set for bushmeat. While undergoing treatment, Taiwo told me about his other twin. He said his Kehinde died, but he kept seeing him every morning before cockcrow. That it was Kehinde that came for him that day in their mother's room, took him out the back door, and led him through a grove behind their outhouse, to show him his new house. More than my uncle, Taiwo scares and confuses me beyond words. Two weeks after his leg was healed, Taiwo's people still did not show up. My uncle waited for three more months, then just made up his mind to allow the boy to attend our primary school. But because Taiwo had never attended school before, my uncle made him start primary one, even though he is three years older than me. At seven years, I was able to teach a ten year-old person arithmetic and handwriting. My uncle saw to it that we went everywhere together. So, he sent the two of us to the farm some three miles away from the village.

On the way to the farm, Taiwo really scared me! He started speaking to somebody, but I could not see anyone. No one. He kept turning this way and that way, as if the person he was addressing kept shifting from the right foot to the left, and back to the right. I kept far away from them both. I couldn't see the other person, but I heard Taiwo tell things about me. He would look at me all the time, at the same time turning this way and that way in the direction of the invisible person.

"Yes, he is a kind boy. No, he too does not have brothers. Yes, I will. No, he won't. He can't see you. What? Stop running. Hey, stop running, Keinde, I need my energy. No, I'm not coming. . . ."

I stayed clear away from Taiwo, and he kept talking to his *ibeji* until we got to the stream, about half-way to the farm. He stopped dead right in front of the stream, looked over his shoulder in my direction, then waved at me. I frowned, wondering why ; but then it came to me: his *ibeji* was leaving. I've heard it said in the village that all twins that have lost their *ibejis* still see them. I too waited on top of the hill and watched Taiwo say something to no one beside his shoulder, then beckoned to me to come over. I rolled up the tip of my khaki trousers before stepping into the warm stream. It reached a little above my shin. Taiwo's khaki shorts were still dry when we dragged our feet out of the warm river.

At the farm, Taiwo and I fetched two baskets of oranges, tangerines and *kolanuts*, then headed back home. On our way back to the village, the clouds turned nasty. It started raining. Thick ugly earthworms slithered all over. The little stream had swollen to Taiwo's knees and way above my waist and while we were wading through it, I stepped on something thick and slimy. I was so sure it was one of those *ojola* pythons that our Nature Studies teacher told us about.. I almost snapped my neck as Taiwo came to my rescue, catching my basket of oranges and tangerines before they could scatter all over the swollen river. I looked back, and saw a fallen banana trunk. By this time, I was already shaking from chills. We trekked the two mile distance home with Taiwo carrying half of my pulped and battered oranges, along with his basket of *kolanuts*.

My teeth chattered all the way home, biting my gum, and the soft part of my mouth. My face felt so hot I was afraid I might lose both eyes. My neck throbbed as if I've just removed a heavy pile of wood I've been carrying on my head and the neck was readjusting. I could feel every bone in my neck creak up. When that happens, something rings a bell in my ears, then half of my face floats above my eyes, only to teasingly settle back. Oh, it hurt so much. . I've never known cold like that afternoon. My whole body was as hot as the bottom of the palm oil mud lamp. It stopped raining few yards away from the village, but I could not help myself; I started crying, and Taiwo didn't trouble himself consoling me. He wasn't even talking to his *ibeji*. He kept silent all the way to my uncle's house.

Mama changed my clothes, and ordered Taiwo to go and rest in our room. My uncle promised to punish us both once he returned from the meeting of elders taking place at the parish house. Teacher Oluwi's sister brought a steaming cup of Ovaltine into my aunt's room for me. Mama thanked her, and put the cup on the wooden table. I reached over and spilled some of the beverage on Mama's special antimacassar. She touched my hair so gently, and said nothing. I didn't think she would beat me because I was shaking so vigorously. She put the cup to my lips, but I couldn't bring my lips together on the aluminum cup because my teeth were chattering so badly. Mama looked at me again, and started crying.

"So, what happened to you at the farm?"

"I-I-I-I ch-ch-ch-ffff-ssstepped on a banana t-t-t—truhnkkkk."

"O to. It's enough. Don't talk. I understand"

D-d—d-d-d-youthi-th-th-think Uncle wi-wwww"

"I said o to. Stop talking. He will not touch you as long as I live. Just go to sleep."

I woke up the next day, still in Mama's bed. It was one of those special mattresses stuffed by the Hausas at the market. They usually mix it with grass and cotton, such that sometime, the fiber sticks out of the thick jute cover. It's still better than plain mats on which we sleep in our room. Taiwo and I sleep in one room, across the hall from Mama's bedroom. There are four rooms in that house. My uncle stays in one room on his own. Teacher Oluwi's sister stays in the adjoining smaller room, with her daughter Keji.

Mama didn't wake me up. She even let me sleep on during the compulsory morning prayer. I don't know what she must have told her husband. Whatever she did tell him, it seemed to work in my favor because when I finally got up, there was not a soul in the house. My uncle must have left very early on his Raleigh bicycle to his dispensary, about five miles from the village. Taiwo would have gone to school, just a stone throw from the house. I opened the wooden window above Mama's *wosiwosi* table. The bright sun made me squint my eyes in pain. I got off the bed by using one of Mama's bags of rice sticking out from under her bed as the step. The hallway has been cleared of yesterday's baskets and spoiled produce. Taiwo must have done my morning chore because I sweep the inside of the house every morning. Keji doesn't do anything. Teacher Oluwi once said that girls must sweep the house. Well, I do all the sweeping in our house. Today is my lucky day since I have no morning chore to do.

There was a bowl of *ogi* and two pieces of *akara* on the table by the hallway where my uncle has fashioned a dining room. He insists people living in his house will not eat their meals inside their sleeping quarters like all the *keferis* that litter the village. So, whatever there is to be eaten, gets eaten around the makeshift dining place along our hallway. The door by this dining place opens directly to the little space I share with Taiwo and his invisible *ibeji*.

I tasted the ogi. Just like I'd imagined; sour beyond compare. The sharpness of the cornmeal rang loud bells in my ears. I dropped the bowl, splattering the *ogi* all over the neatly swept floor. I left the mess there, in the middle of the room, changed into my khaki shorts and cotton shirt uniform, and left for school.

Teacher Oluwi was standing by the door, fondling the caning stick, when I entered my classroom. It was as if he was waiting for me. The pupils were seated in their chairs, eyes eager with expectation. I stood by the door, right in front of the teacher, my eyes fixed on the shiny cane.

"And why are you late?"

"I am sorry sir"

"It's not a matter of 'sorry sir'; where were you twenty minutes ago?"

"In my uncle's house, sir"

"And where, I pray is your uncle?"

"Sir, he has gone to the dispensary sir"

"Oh, I see. And why were you not in school on time?"

"Because..I . . . I am ..sir, I did not wake up in time ..sorry sir"

"And why, I pray? Young man, why did you oversleep?"

"It's the fever, sir. I think I have the high Fahrenheit, sir"

"You have fever?"

"Yes sir; the high one. The big Fahrenheit sir"

"Come here . . ."(He touched my face; instantly removing his hands).

"Jesusofnazareth!"

"Sorry sir"

"Sorry, my foot; ahholymariamotherofgod!!"

"I'm sorry sir"

"Quiet, boy. You are very ill. Go right now to your house. Tell that stingy uncle of yours to take you to a decent hospital. Hey-eh-eh *omolomo*. *O mase o*. What a pity"

And so he sent me home

When I got back home, my aunt was in the kitchen outside, cooking the school lunch for that day. When she saw me, she stopped fanning the smoky firewood. Tongues of orange flame erupted and she placed a huge pot of water on the *aaro*. She wiped the smoke from her teary eyes, and pulled me into her warm embrace.

"*Jesumimo olugbala araiye!*" She exclaimed, releasing me immediately. Since I wasn't expecting such an abrupt reaction, I dropped on the dirt floor, watching Mama's feet come out of the plastic slippers. Her little toe rested on the kitchen floor, while the others seemed to dance on top of the slippers.

"Ola, come. Why did you get up from the bed?"

"I wanted to go to school"

"Did you know you were very ill yesterday?"

"I—I"

"Don't worry, *Omo;* go now and sit in my room while I look for Baba Keji."

"Mama?"

"Yes, my son?"

"Are you taking me to the city?"

"Eh-ehhh-eeh, who said so?"

"Nobody—just Teacher Oluwi."

"I've told you not to listen to anything your teacher tells you that has nothing to do with A-B-D or 1-2-3. You hear me?"

"Mama, he he ..the teacher said to tell Baba to take me to a proper hospital."

"O-ho . . . He said that?"

"Yes, mama. He wants me to be taken to a proper hospital, where they will know what to do with big big Fahrehnheit."

"Fareti..? What is this child saying, *Jesu?*"

"Mama, that is what people get when they have fever."

"You have fever alright; you are not making any sense right now. Do as I said: go and lay down while I look for the *oloriburuku* one here. You hear me?"

I made my way to her room, wondering why Mama just called her husband a bad name, using a word we are all forbidden to use in the house. I know sometimes my uncle deserves to be called names, but never from my aunt. She once washed the mouth of one of our neighbors' children with soda water. Tunde, the nine year-old was heard to have called Keji's mother a bad name; a very very bad name. He and Keji were playing outside the dispensary one day, and my aunt had gone with Taiwo to clean his sore and was waiting outside the dispensary, by the little lawn when she heard Tunde call Keji a bad name. Keji was said to have erased the line drawn by Tunde on the sand, signifying that something bad would happen to his mother. But that would have been true only if an ant had crawled over the line, and according to Keji, she got tired of waiting for an ant to crawl across the line, so she kicked some dirt over the line, thus erasing it. To Tunde, that meant instant death for his mother. Keji bolted as soon as she realized what she had done, and it was while he was chasing her that Tunde, out of frustration shouted "Your mother!" as he spread out his fingers at Keji. That was when Mama saw him, and dragged him inside the dispensary where they were bandaging Taiwo's leg. She scooped soapy water from one of the bowls on a wooden table, ignored my uncle's questioning look and wiped Tunde's face with the suds. He screamed and struggled free of my aunt's grip, and ran out of the dispensary.

"I thought I asked you to lie down?"

Mama appeared in the room, looking perplexed at me, still in my school uniform. I had forgotten what she asked me to do; apparently I was carried away by that incident with Keji and Tunde. I remember she said she was going to look for the *olori*, ehm, my uncle. But she should remember that he must still be at the dispensary. I allowed my hand to be held in Mama's work calloused one. My face floated in front of me, as if leading me somewhere. The back of my neck hurt so much. I withdrew my hand from Mama's grip. She looked at me, rubbed her hands together, and snapped the fingers. She did that only when she was disturbed about something, or when my uncle said something bad to her.

My head floated up and met my face in front of Mama's oval mirror by her big fluffy bed. I saw her pull out some drawers under the looking glass and rummaged inside. As she was checking the contents of envelopes of assortments of medicine bought from peddlers inside Idogo train, my aunt kept talking to no one.

"Hey-eh, Sade, you won't look on and allow your only child to die like this? Hehhn, where is this medicine now? Folasade, please, save your little son. Look at him, he is ill. Save him"

My face left the space behind my aunt's head-tie, and floated back to my chest. I tried to understand what my aunt was saying. Who is going to die? Not me, I hope. But she was talking to my mother! Sade is the name of my mother. And she is dead. Bells rang inside my right ear. My left one has been blocked by the heat that seemed to be boiling the left side of my head.

Look at him. Poor boy. What has he ever done to anybody? See the animal that calls himself his father. What has he done to save him? And he calls himself a Christian. Ah, Jesumaria, help me with this boy. I need money to take him to Ikeja. But first, I must get him out of this house. I need a lorry. Oh, help me Sade. That is your son. Help.

I heard the door shut. There were envelopes scattered all over the floor in my aunt's room. I was still lying in her bed, covered with layers and layers of *aran*, *aso-oke* and other thick wrappers. The smell of camphor was heady, stinging my eyes. My neck hurt so much. My uncle once told me that people with extra neckbone like mine have tough luck in life. He said headaches would be our constant companion, and that when boys grew up to be men, they would look ungainly with long necks like giraffe. Well, my long giraffe neck now hurt as if I've been hit with an *apola* that my aunt cooks her special food with.

The door opened and I heard more feet rush in. The layers of clothes were peeled off by I don't-know-who. All I know was that I found myself shaking uncontrollably.

"See, he has the chills"

"Poor boy, it is fever"

"Did he get his own *nomba* ?"

"Ah, he was to get it but his uncle felt he was too little"

"Too little my foot! How old does he think they inoculate children nowadays?"

"Remove those piles of *aso*. Ah-ha, doesn't anyone know anything about fever in this house?"

"By the way, Mama Ola, where is Baba Keji?"

"Are you all deaf, I told you I couldn't find him in his dispensary. He probably has left for Agege to buy some medicines for the dispensary."

"Ola!"

"Ola!!"

"Ola, good boy, wake up!!!"

The chills started from my head, rested a moment by my cheeks, then traveled down to the back of my neck, where they trickled down to my shoulders and chest. There, at last was where they found abode. They all sat around the little spaces in my chest. One of the chills kicked the lower jaw of my face, making my teeth clatter, chatter, clatter. My face got tired of floating about, and settled permanently somewhere between my head and the wall While all that commotion was going on, my back ached and I tried stretching myself to relieve the discomfort. Unfortunately, each time I attempted shifting my position in my aunt's bed, my back refused to cooperate, and would snap back to the uncomfortable position. It felt as if I were an *eja sawa* that has been roasted to a permanent twisted shape. My stomach kept gurgling and making so much noise that would have embarrassed me to no end in front of Teacher Oluwi's class.

The bed sank. Someone was sitting on the edge. Mama spoke from a space by the wall next to my face.

"We are going to take you to the hospital in the city"

I tried to talk, but my voice was still inside my stomach. The camphor smell was gone, but has been replaced by the unmistakable odor of freshly squeezed bitter leaf juice. The person sitting by the edge of Mama's bed stood up and the bed shifted to one side, as if it was being rocked by someone. Mama lifted the pillow behind my head. My neck felt constricted and stretched to an unnatural length as my head was lowered onto an aluminum cup. Strong bitterleaf juice smell drenched my nostrils and I threw up before my lips touched the dark green liquid. Digested remnants of the *ogi* and *akara* that I ate few hours before spattered all over Mam's fluffy bed and nice mud wall. Slimy fluid trickled down from the antimacassar table cloth onto the Bible on top of the pillow next to my head.

"See what you have done"

"Why are you behaving like a baby?"

"Ola, what is wrong with you, drink that up"

"You want to get well? Then drink that thing up"

"Mama Ola, give me that wrapper. We have to wipe this mess from his ears"

Blobs and globs of slimy yellowish thing drained from my mouth, nose and the cup. Feet rushed in and out. Voices cursed my uncle in different pitches. Mama lowered me back on a remade bed. The camphor was not strong enough to disguise nauseating smell of my vomit in the room. People rushed out with hurriedly dispensed pieces of advice to my aunt.

"This is more than you can manage on your own, Mama Ola"

"You'd better take this child to Ikeja o"

"At least to Arigbajo"

"Look, Iya Ola, we'll lend you money if that's a problem"

"Or, one of us can go with you . . ."

I didn't think anyone should go with me to the hospital

Feet rushed back inside the room. Voices boomed and bounced about my face. My ears ached with every sound. The voices floated and danced around my head, opening up and teasing the bone inside my head, rising up and down, up and down, round and round, and then up.

Iya Ola, bad news

What is it

They said the bridge collapsed

What bridge..You don't mean the one to the

Yes, the very same one. Your husband can't even come back into the village

But what about this poor boy

Isn't that what we've been trying to tell you

There is no way a lorry can get here. The only way is through that bridge. Now, it's broken

Whoever heard of such nonsense. A broken bridge.

Why not? Didn't you hear that the Fulani herdsmen weakened that bridge? How?

Are you new to this area? Those cattlemen herded their animals, all two hundred of them, over a rickety wooden bridge.

And we all pay tax o, ehn? We paid tax, and see what those foolish oselus have given us, a broken bridge.

People, all these iregbes won't help Ola. We need to take him to the big hospital in the city.

How will we get him there?

On Iya Ola's back. Ah-ha, what does that child weigh? A cheap bag of tobacco is heavier and some women have walked to the marketplace with that balanced on their heads. Oya, Iya Ola, let us get this boy to

Stop there! Where are you taking him? Ah-ha. Before the days of needles inside human skin, ah-ha, didn't people cure their illness? All of you, leave me and his mother in this room, and I will prove to you that the we have been curing iba long before the whiteman brought his medicines and needles.

I don't know how long I stayed in that room. When I next opened my eyes, Mama was sitting on a small stool by her own bed, on which I was lying. I had been stripped to the skin. I sat up. And fell back instantly. She rose from the stool and reached her arms to help me up. I still could not get up. I did not want to. I was so tired it felt as if I'd emptied my stomach of everything I'd been eating and drinking since I was born. It was as if my stomach was a huge pumpkins whose insides had been emptied of its seeds. There was a great urge to eat. Steam wafted from one of the bowls. The aroma of my favorite *akara* generated a cascade of saliva from under my tongue, and behind the walls of my cheeks. I heaved, my sides ached, I felt a drop of urine inside my under pant, and threw up nothing. I swallowed bitter saliva. I wonder if they probably forced some bitter leaf juice down my throat while I was asleep.

My throat constricted. I couldn't swallow. It felt as if I had a bad sore. I tried swallowing again, working the drooling stuff past my tongue which already felt heavy and thick. But the fleshy part of my cheeks redirected the saliva through the only path which was by now a swollen raw piece of flesh hanging from the roof of my mouth. I gave up and the saliva drooled all over my shoulders and armpits. I reached out my hands to wipe the mess. Then I saw them. Rashes! The back of my hands were covered in spots.

Mama left to look for a rag to wipe the drool off my body. She didn't appear surprised because she just looked at me and left the room. As she left, I rolled my eyes to the space next to the antimacassar table where Mama's looking glass is. I heaved myself up on my elbows and saw a boy who looked like me trying to see himself in the mirror. The boy opened his mouth, still poised on his thin elbows, and looked in the mirror. Red spots on the sore tongue, all over the length of that cavernous mouth. Red red spots.

I sank back into Mama's fluffy bed. The boy in the mirror vanished , and I saw the spots all splashed on the glass. Spots here and there. Flat and blubbery spots. Red, flat dots all over Mama's mirror.

Mama entered, accompanied by one of my uncle's best friends. His name is Omoawo. My uncle calls him EF, for something Fatunde. But little people like me call the man Papa. Just that. Papa. It shows we respect him. I don't know why they call him Omoawo when his name is something Fatunde. He is the same man who showed my uncle different ways old people cured assorted diseases before people like my uncle went to fight in wars they had no idea why. I could tell it was Papa, not because I saw him first. No, my aunt came in first, then Papa. But I smelled him before I saw him. He always carried a worn out bag made of some animal skin. Must not be cow, because the skin on Papa's bag shone anytime rain or any kind of water fell on it. The strap is made of snake skin. I know that because I have seen different snake skins under rocks around the village, and on the farm. Taiwo once told me that snakes changed their skins anytime they got tired of wearing the same thing. I even took one of such and showed it to Mama, but she screamed and made me throw it away.

Papa muttered something when he saw me. He chanted the *oriki* of Soponna, the god of Smallpox. It sounded like *Elegbana.* . . . Something like that.

May be that's what I have! Smallpox!! Small..!!! Oh my God. No wonder I am dying. The old man's wrinkled face dropped on mine and the bag slung over the wizened old figure gave off such strong odor that Teacher Oluwi would probably have found offensive; but in a strange way, I've grown to like it because Papa always have something nice for me. He gave me a smoked fish the last time he was in our house. He stared deeply in my eyes. His gaze weakened my eyelids. They shut closed.

"Ola, my child"

I tried answering, but my voice still sat inside my stomach. He moved nearer the bed, and sat on the stool Mama always used. He set down his bag. Fresh odor of a medley of roasted bush meat, ground tobacco leaf, gun powder, and sweat filled the space under my nose.

"You have to eat something. You hear me?"

I swallowed. Nothing happened. That means I could not swallow anything because my throat was raw and very sore. Mama wiped the saliva streaming down my ears. She opened one of the bowls by the foot of the bed. I smelled the fresh aroma of snail fried in onion and *atarodo*

"Iya Ola, don't give him this. He cannot swallow anything solid. Go and make some liquid drink, like *ogi* for him."

Mama explained that she already tried that with me, and I vomited everything. She started crying, but the old man assured her that he would help cure me. He told my aunt that she should make sure nobody enter the room for the next three weeks, since I might become highly infectious. He ordered her to bring freshly laid eggs, palm oil, palm wine, and freshly squeezed bitter leaf. I started crying when I heard that, knowing that they would force the bitter liquid down my raw, sore throat.

My aunt left to procure all the things Papa listed for her.

While she was gone, Papa rummaged in his bag, and started sorting things in front of him. He rose to his feet, moved near the bed, and touched my face with some powder. It smelled like dried chicken poop. I felt the poop dissolve on my face as I was sweating profusely. Papa muttered his Soponna song again, smiling as he confirmed that I indeed was suffering from smallpox. He wiped my face and his hands felt like dried leather being dragged across my face. I shut my eyes.

When I woke up, Papa was gone, so was Mama. There was nobody around, although I could hear people's voices from behind the door. I listened hard for my uncle's raspy croak, but his was absent. Probably he hasn't come back from Agege. I wanted so much to ask questions. I wanted to know for how long I was going to be in that room all by myself. I wanted to ask somebody if Teacher Oluwi had been informed of my condition. I wanted to stand in front of the whole class 3B and inform them proudly, that I have smallpox, but did not die. Most of all, I wondered where Mama was, and how come she had not popped in to see me. I don't remember when I last saw her for that matter. It must have been when she brought in all those things Papa asked her to. May be I saw it in my dream, but I remember seeing my aunt come in with all those things in one of the baskets one of her friends wound for her.

Papa took the eggs from her. There were seven of them. He broke three, and dropped the yellow yolks into a plastic cup. It was one of those cups my uncle brought back from one of his meetings in Arigbajo. I t had the picture of one old man all over it. My uncle would not allow anybody to use this cup, but here it was, in the hands of the village herbalist. Thinking about my uncle made me wonder where he could be. I could not say for how long he had been away. But judging from my illness, I would think at least one week. Papa told me he'd been trying to make me eat since I got ill one week ago. That was how I knew that my uncle had been away for a whole week.

"Ola, you must drink this. It's something for your illness."

I prayed he was not going to make me put my mouth near that cup. He stirred the mixture again, and I saw the blobs of white sticking to the edge of the cup. He added some salt, and stirred again.

"See? It's not going to taste that badly. Just try it."

I tried opening my mouth. This time I could. Involuntarily, my throat clamped shut. The mixture was so sickening. I swallowed, and this time, it did not hurt as much as before. The man put one talisman-laden hand behind my head, and lifted the cup to my lips with the other. I willed the lips to open, but nothing happened. He went back and sat on his stool. I fell back on Mama's fluffy bed. By this time, the spots on my body had spread everywhere, including way inside my underpants. They looked like hundreds and hundreds of raised bumps on a shiny reddish-brown surface. Like lots of black-eyed beans with the black eyes being pus-filled. For the first time, I noticed that I was covered all over with palm oil. Palm oil! The same oil Mama cooked my favorite *efo oniru* and fried snail with. My skin looked like a leopard skin; only a leopard's skin is not bumpy. I crawled at the sight.

The old man ordered me to stick out my tongue. I did, and it did not feel that sore anymore. I swallowed the thick salty yolk. I just thought of Taiwo eating a tasty bowl of fried snail, and it didn't seem that bad. I was then given some spoonfuls of the same oil to drink. In a strange way, it didn't taste as awfully as I had anticipated. He told me I would do the same thing in a few hours. He must have come back several times, because I lost count, and one thing led to another, and before I knew it, I had got used to gulping the salty yolk, followed by the freshly–tapped palm wine mixed with bitter leaf juice. That, according to my aunt was the regimen recommended for smallpox, and but for that good old man, I would have been dead before her *oloriburuku* husband returned from the city.

Of all the smelly and tasteless things they forced me to eat and drink, my favorite throughout those lonely three weeks was the palm wine mixed with bitter leaf juice. When I first drank it, I told you I threw up. The *ewuro* shocked the fermented sourness out of the potion that all I tasted was bitterness that shook the roots of my mouth, and pushed goose pimples from the depths of my bumpy skin. The next time I was given the mixture, my hunger pang had lost its shame, and I was ready to eat anything that would fill up my famished stomach. I thought I was going to die when Papa raised the smelly aluminum cup to my face. I did not; instead I found myself swallowing and tasting sour palm-wine. The only bad thing about drinking that fermented potion is I belched a lot. And the gas was nauseous! Even then, I soon got used to the stench of constipated fumes. I also slept all the time.

Of all the lonely time I spent in that room, I will never forget nighttime. In the morning, Mama would call my name from behind the door. At the end of the first week when the bumps on my skin felt like a group of small hills spread out on a flat valley, Papa told me that I was going to be on my own for two more weeks. Then I didn't even realize that I had been on my own in that room for three whole days. He told me I slept through all those days.

There was a time when I thought I saw my mother. I opened my eyes, and there she was, smiling kindly at me, right on top of the antimacassar table. Every time she smiled, my eyes dimmed, closed shut and seemed to walk backwards inside my skull. Yes, you heard me right; I saw my eyes roll backwards, like when we play the *ikoto* on the sand. They walked backwards, backwards, until they hit the back of my head *gbaga!* Just like that. Anytime one eyeball rolled to the very back of my skull, my ears exploded into shrills, squeaks and *gbinrirn-gbinrin* sound Teacher Oluwi's bell makes anytime he shakes it irritably. Then I would see my mother's face smiling benevolently at me, from the top of the antimacassar table where my aunt usually keeps her picture. I wanted to tell her to stop smiling, and simply go away, as her kindness was not doing me any good. I must have finally fallen asleep after refusing to open my eyes;

well, I could not do anything with them since the eyeballs just stayed at the back, and would not do a return trip to the front of my face.

It was so weird!

All the time in that room, I longed to have company, but nobody showed up. With the exception of Papa who called from behind the door to announce his entrance, no one else visited me while I fought the rolling eyeballs, the screaming eardrums and the unbelievably hot blanket of skin that covered me up. My skin felt alive all the time. It was as if someone emptied a basket of hairy insects, like the ones that dropped off the cotton tree on the path way to the village stream. Those ones always give me the creeps. Once, on my way from fetching a pot of water, seven of those things, as long as my middle finger dropped into my pot, making *plonk-plonk-plonk-shrrr* noise as they hit the water. I remember yelling and dropping my waterpot, and running all the way to my uncle's house. He almost sent me back to refill the water but for my aunt who insisted she had to rub coconut oil on the bites all over my arm left by the crawly caterpillars. I shudder now as I recall the event. Nothing pushes the goose pimples to the surface of my skin like the thought of those cursed insects in their sickening colorful swarm eating up a whole tree in less than a week.

My skin looked strange all the time I was in that room. Whenever Papa came in, he would rub something that I eventually discovered was palm-oil all over me. The first time I noticed him do this, my skin felt so sore, raw and blistery. When next I was conscious enough to observe, I noticed that the raised bumps that trapped something whitish underneath their shiny covers, now seemed flattened. The fluid inside the blisters had also drained through the opened cover. It reminds me of that time in our science class when Teacher Oluwi told us about the top of mountains that got flattened because of fires raging underneath them. That is how my skin's new surface looks like.

At first, the rashes did not hurt; I was merely uncomfortable. The thought of not being able to swallow, or the mere sight of those wart like formations on my tongue and the blisters that decorate the back of my ears, my face, including my eyelids, the whole of my back, all over my stomach that for a long time, I did not see my navel;—ugghhh! It's nauseating thinking about it—all that captivate my mind that if there was any pain, I did not feel it on those first few days. However, things changed when I stopped falling asleep. I began feeling the discomfort. Papa's native medicine shocked the caterpillars from crawling all over my skin; instead they just turned and urinated on me. That was how it felt whenever the native doctor poured one potion after another on my scaly skin oozing thick grayish-cream fluid from under those raised bumps. When the tops of those mountains dropped, the surprised cover sank onto the skin underneath, spreading an incredibly stinging heat all over my body. The sensation was not the kind you could relieve by scratching, or rubbing; what I did was pretend I was in a room with Taiwo where we were enjoying a bowl of fried snails, and my aunt's favorite vegetable soup loaded with dried shrimp and *eja osan* and locust beans. By the time we finished our huge bowl of pounded cocoyam, the unbelievable sting was over. Sometime, I lost the chance to imagine, especially when Papa came in and poured all sorts of liquids, potions, and powdery concoctions all over me.

By the end of the second week since I became ill first with the big Fahrenheit, and then the smallpox, Papa came into my aunt's room where I'd been living all the time. He brought his little earthen pots. I started getting better when the scabs on my skin turned to scaly flakes. At first, the rashes itched and I would scratch and scratch until the scabs fall off. The first time I scratched, brownish liquid and water oozed out of the scab. Then it dried and really itched, and I enjoyed scratching. You should see the scars those poxes left! All over my back, at the base of my neck. I have at least thirteen that pattern the back of my hands. Even my feet were not spared. The spots on the two resemble the design etched in some of Pa Faleye's sculptors. It's as if Pa Faleye used some of his instruments to carve out little dots around my feet. I had no facial marks when I was born, but the mirror in Mama's room shows me a face cicatriced with strange marks. The ones below my eyebrows are shaped like the letter 'Y', with the two arms sitting on my nose. Mama says I look like an *abiku*. Two hollowed dots below my chin create an artificial dimple. I look so horrible. But Mama told me not to worry about my face.

I don't know what happened to my uncle. I've been on my bed since the day I got sick. Mama told me all the things that had happened in school. How some of my friends form my class sent their greetings during lunch break; how one child had got trampled at the marketplace while children were waiting in unbelievable heat for some " foolish *oselu*" to arrive from Lagos; how she is now happy I didn't have to join the unfortunate group in the market, and so on. Most of all, I wanted to find where my uncle is. Not because I am enamored of him; but the curiosity of what could have happened to him on a rickety bridge got the better of me and I heard my voice ask "Where is Baba?"

My aunt did not answer me, she just looked at me, hissed and said, "He is fine." Three more days, and Baba still did not show up. When they allowed me to leave my room, my legs were so light that I fell right back on Mama's bed.

Right now, I am waiting for Papa to come in with the things he had collected for my washing. He told Mama I had to be washed thoroughly so that the *Elegbara* would not visit me again. I wanted to ask why Smallpox needed to 'visit' anyone at all. Doesn't it realize that people found it repulsive? I wanted to ask so many questions but Papa walked in, dragging a whole branch of some tree with him. He told me Mama would have to boil the leaves for tea for me. The bark of the wood, she would scrape and soak in a special bottle that already had different medicines prepared. Finally, I was never to wear any of the things my body touched during my three-week of illness.

Mama walks in, looking much happier than I've ever seen her in all the years I've lived in her house.

"You are cured. Ola, you are now well. Thank God"

"But, am I still going to the hospital?"

"Hospital ke, *otio*, no hospital. From now on, whenever your *oloriburuku* uncle returns from wherever he has traveled, you will go for check-ups at the dispensary. Taiwo will go with you whenever I'm selling food."

"Ah, Mmaa maa"

"Why are you crying, my son? Ehn, don't you see that there is no need to go to Lagos again?"

"Mama, I really want to go to the big hospital.. I truly want to. They have toys for children. And lots of good things."

"That's all? Ehn, just toys? Don't worry, I'll get you fine fine toys from the market, *s'o gbo?*"

I was not listening. I saw myself climbing those metal steps, and entering a long hallway at the end of which stood a kind looking nurse, holding a basket full of toys, waiting to lead me to a clean room with a whole bed just for myself. A real hospital.

GLOSSARY OF NIGERIAN (YORUBA) WORDS

Abiku.   Among the Yorubas of Nigeria, a child that dies and returns to the same mother to be born again.

Akara.   Bean fritters

Apola.   A piece of hewn log used for cooking

Aran.   Velvety cloth favored among the Yoruba

Aso-oke.   Piece of textile locally loomed.

Atarodo.   Habanero pepper

Efo oniru.   Vegetable dish flavored with dried fish and local spice.

Elegbara.   One of the praise names of Soponna, the Yoruba god of Smallpox.

Eja osan.   Sun-dried fish used in special delicacies.

Eja sawa.   Bony dried fish

Gbaga.   Yoruba for a Thud-like sound.

Gbinrin.   Yoruba for the clanging of bell

Ikoto.   Local toy made from the shells of small snails
Jesumimo olugbala araiye!   "Holy Jesus the Savior of the World!"
Oriki.   Praise name
Omo.   Child
Omolomo.   Somebody's child
O mase o.   What a pity
Ketekete.   Donkey
Petes.   Multi-storey building
Keferi.   Non-believers; anyone who does not believe in the Christian or Muslim God.
Nomba.   Vaccination

www.ingramcontent.com/pod-product-compliance
Lightning Source LLC
Chambersburg PA
CBHW030654110726
47901CB00002B/719